THE SLOW WAVE

THE SLOW WAVE

Robert Paget

Copyright © 2023 Robert Paget. All rights reserved.

No part of this book may be reproduced or transmitted in any form or by any means, graphic, electronic, or mechanical, including photocopying, recording, taping, or by any information storage retrieval system, without the permission, in writing, of the publisher. For more information, send an email to support@sbpra.net, Attention: Subsidiary Rights.

Strategic Book Publishing
www.sbpra.net

For information about special discounts for bulk purchases, please contact Strategic Book Publishing, Special Sales, at bookorder@sbpra.net.

ISBN: 978-1-68235-880-1

For Iris

'Life is a Dream'

Virginia Woolf

- 1 -

The first thing Bud Turner saw when he hit the coastal road was the light blue tranquil waters of Lauderdale Beach. A blanket of pristine white sand disappeared up the coast into the distance. Single story, Art Deco buildings fronted the beach. Their bold architecture reminiscent of a bygone era. A combination of bars, motels, souvenir shops, and inexpensive restaurants. Fitzgerald's Jazz Age forever present.

Girls clad only in the miniest of bikinis blanketed the beach; water soothed the rest. Cars of all descriptions lined the beachfront reflecting the sun into Bud's eyes. Taking off his sunglasses and carefully putting them on the dashboard of his MGB sports car, he took the towel lying on the seat and wiped the perspiration from his face. The heat was oppressive, the humidity stifling. The scorching sun had already darkened his sallow complexion in the two days he had been on the road. The beach drew college youth from all over the country.

The sun's reflection off the hood of the MG blurred his vision. He made a quick recovery before slamming into the car in front of him. Something else caught his attention; blonde, long-legged, willowy bodies of two very nubile coeds. *If this is what it's going to be like, I'm all for it*, he thought to himself.

He kept his attention on them as they crossed in front of his car and disappeared into a sun-tinted window bar, as if swallowed up by the dark. The neon sign above read, "The Sand Box."

Sudden honking broke his attention. He continued down Highway A1A, eyes darting to the beach occasionally, looking for more nubile bodies.

***

Home wasn't like this. Ames, Iowa couldn't be, even though it was a college town.

College produced no direction for him. No interests. He left to find out if his existence held more than the middle-class life that was stifling him.

"If you leave, you leave without my blessing," his father said. Those were the last words he heard from him.

His mother understood. Bud's situation was similar to hers: being somewhere she didn't want to be, tied down to a life and man she no longer loved—a man who had changed so drastically she wasn't sure it was the same man she married.

"I have to get away," he said to Sheila, his girlfriend, before he left.

Sheila tenderly kissed him, tears welling her eyes, full of sadness that her first love was leaving.

***

The surf was inviting. He pulled his MGB into a vacant space under one of the hundreds of palms trees lining the road as far as the eye could see. He took his swimsuit and towel from his carryall, made sure his trunk was locked, hid the car keys under the dashboard, and headed for the concrete building on the beach marked "MEN."

The bracing water didn't displace the exhaustion he felt from the long drive. He headed for his towel, which he'd placed on the sand not far from his car. Strolling by, casual as habitual beach residents, two bikini-clad nubile bodies. They noticed him staring, smiled, and continued on. He toweled dry, keeping his eyes on them as they continued their beach promenading.

"Nice, eh?" a deep resonant voice said, knowing what the kid standing in front of him was thinking. He'd seen that predatory look on many neophyte Ft. Lauderdale college kids. A word to the wise sometimes helped before they found themselves in trouble. He knew all the usual beautiful female residents who used the beach. He prided himself on keeping them out of trouble also. The two that just passed were not only residents, but were part of the regular beach crowd, which comprised the lifeguards, their girlfriends, and the local residents. It was a small eclectic group. He wasn't sure who these two were attached to, but he didn't need any trouble with his lifeguards or the beach crowd. It was best to be safe than sorry. It was prudent to keep the visiting firemen from the habitues.

The white patch on his red trunks read, "Ft. Lauderdale Beach Patrol." He looked old for a lifeguard, maybe early forties or more. His grinning, weather-beaten face was lined permanently from years under the sun. Bud nodded yes, turning his gaze back to the objects of discussion.

"There's many more like that around here. You'll find out for yourself. Best to keep to the transient college variety rather than the residents," the guard said.

"Thanks," Bud said, sensing the admonition in the advice. He wasn't here for confrontation, physical or verbal. He let the informative conversation end and sat on his towel, ignoring the guard and any further advice forthcoming.

- 2 -

"Hey, hey, wake up." Bud opened his eyes to see the same guard from before was standing over him. "You must've had a long trip."

Bud rubbed his eyes and sat up, not knowing how long he'd been asleep. "Yeah. Two days on the road. All the way from Iowa. What time is it?" He'd left his watch with his clothes in the trunk of the MGB.

"Five thirty. You've been asleep since three. Dangerous. You were lucky it clouded over. Sun can really burn if you're not use to it."

There was no rebuke in his words as before, just straight forward, good neighborly advice. There was even a faint smile on his chiseled face. If he was being helpful, maybe he could help him further.

"Thanks. Again."

Bud got to his feet. The guard towered over him at least another five or six inches, and Bud was six feet tall.

"Maybe you know a place to stay. Nothing fancy," Bud said.

"What's your budget?" the guard asked.

"All I need is a place to sleep. As I said, nothing fancy."

"Off the top of my head, I have no idea. But go over to The Sand Box. Ask for Max. He may be able to help you."

"The Sand Box?"

"Across from number 7 lifeguard stand. Make a U-turn and head down a few blocks. You can't miss it." He headed off down the beach, searching the surf as he did.

"Hey, what's your name in case Max asks who told me?"

"Dough," he called back, breaking into a slow jog.

Nice guy, Bud thought. If everyone down here is as nice as that, he had made the right decision in coming to Ft. Lauderdale.

※※※

Being around his father's constant criticism about not doing his best was emotionally draining. And it undermined his confidence. Sometimes he felt there was nothing he could do that would please his father, or that he could do anything right at all. It constrained him to the point where he was hesitant to ask questions, about anything. The only solace came from his mother, who watched silently as tempers flared and arguments ensued. He knew she would endure the confrontations hoping for no physical violence. Yes, they both carried the same burdens, and frustrations, of micromanagement and insensitivity to all things not in the oppressive quiver of their dominant overseer. Luckily, he had the choice to leave. His mother had to endure. She had been under his dominating influence for years. Her self-confidence had eroded years ago. It was one of the reasons there were no more children. She made sure of that. She would not go through the same torment she had with Bud. He had often wondered how it started. Two compatible people meet, fall in love, have a child, and then the marriage disintegrates. Why? Right now, he was the free entity in the equation. In time he would try to alleviate his mother's plight.

※※※

"I'd better wash this little gem," he said to himself looking at his MGB. The trip had put a layer of heavy grime over the fire-engine red body. He took his keys from their hiding place under the dashboard, started the almost silent motor, and executed a U-turn, first checking his rear, making sure not to become a statistic. Sliding the MGB into a parking space in front of The Sand Box, he pulled on his T-shirt and followed the throbbing music into the darkness.

"ID."

Except for the dim light penetrating the tinted window and the multicolored lights from the throbbing juke box, the interior was almost opaque. It took a moment for his eyes to adjust. An attractive, tall, suntanned bartender with long blonde hair past her shoulders who looked to be in her early twenties nonchalantly stood behind the bar, looking straight at Bud.

"What?" he said loudly over the music.

"ID," she said again.

"It's in the car ... but I'm over twenty-one. I was born in forty-six," he said smiling.

"You might be over twenty-one. And you may have been born in forty-six, but how old are you?" she asked without a hint of irony.

"That doesn't make sense," Bud said, smiling. "I ..."

"I believe you, but the state may not. If you haven't got ID on you, you can't stay."

"I'll be right back."

He took his wallet from his denims and went back into The Sand Box.

"Here." He held his license out to the girl.

"What do you want?" she asked, ignoring it.

"Beer. Any kind."

He sat on one of the wooden barstools lining the bar. A fishnet hung from the ceiling, falling over most of the back wall behind the bar. It was decorated with seashells and pieces of driftwood. The walls housed beer advertisements and more driftwood, which was evidently nailed to it. Two beer spigots with beer mugs beside them were built into the center of the bar counter, where another fishnet hung from the ceiling. Bud was surprised by the absence of liquor bottles. This was a bar, after all, but not one liquor bottle was evident. Other than the fetid beer stench, there was nothing to indicate it was.

"Twenty-five," the blonde said, leaning on the bar.

Bud handed her a dollar bill, watching as she made change.

"Is Max around?" he asked.

"No. He left." She laid his change on the bar.

"That's too bad. I was hoping he could help me find a place to stay."

"You just here for the summer?" she asked blandly.

"If you mean, am I visiting? Yes. But I'm planning to stay a while."

"I'm Bev. If you're looking for a place, go over and ask Scotty, at the end of the bar."

"Thanks. I'm Bud."

He watched as she walked away. She turned, sensing him looking at her and smiled. She was surprised that she blurted out her name to a total stranger. She'd never done that before, especially to anyone coming into The Box.

"See what I mean?"

Bud turned, meeting Dough's grinning face.

"I told you there was plenty of that around here."

"How right you are."

Bud was looking at a face full of experience. The eyes rheumy, obviously a drinker, but full of concern.

"Did you find Max?" Dough asked.

"No. He's not here. Bev suggested I talk to Scotty."

"Yeah, he's a beach bum. He'll know a place."

Bev came over, placed a beer in front of Dough, and left. But not before eyeballing Bud, the smile still on her lips. Dough couldn't help but notice it. His grin turned into a self-pleasing smile. Bud also sensed the change and screwed up his mouth in puzzlement. Was she hitting on him? No. Impossible. His imagination was working overtime. Although it was a pleasant thought.

"After a while she'll know what beer you drink before you ask for it. And judging from that look she gave you, it won't take long," Dough said.

"Really? How long is that?" Bud asked.

"Not long, as I said." Dough finished his beer in one long gulp, placed the empty glass on the bar, and was rewarded with another.

He gulped down most of it. Bud knew this guy was a heavy drinker. Bev wiped down the bar in front of them, although it wasn't necessary.

"Bev knows when to bring them without asking." He winked at her, acknowledging her expertise. She demurred with a playful sneer and left. "When she does ask, I know it's time to stop." A tinge of melancholy surrounded his words.

"I should speak to Scotty," Bud said, rising from the barstool.

"Stay, I'll call him over. Hey Scotty!" Dough shouted over the music and waved him over.

A powerfully built man came from the other end of the bar. Identical in every way to Dough, same age range, over six feet tall, blond, deeply tanned, with a heavily lined face, wearing red trunks with a patch that read, "Ft. Lauderdale Beach Patrol." Even the rheumy eyes held the same enigmatic quality.

"This is …" Dough started to say.

"Bud."

"Bud," he finished. "He's looking for a place. Nothing fancy."

Scotty stuck out a paw-like hand and shook Bud's as if he was mashing pulp. "How long you here for?" he asked.

"I'm not sure. The summer at least. Maybe longer."

"There's a place over on Las Olas, Casa Jacaranda. I don't know if it's free, but he can try. Has a bedroom, kitchen, bath …" Scotty said.

"Wait a minute. I said nothing fancy. That sounds like it'll run into plenty," Bud responded.

Scotty didn't wait for Bud to finish. He headed for the other end of the bar, stopping to talk to a girl who just came in. Together they walked to the end of the bar, where Scotty had been sitting with another girl, just as striking as any Bud had already seen. Ft. Lauderdale seemed to be inhabited by nothing but beautiful young women who could just as easily be glamorous models or film stars.

Bev came up with another beer for Dough as he was finishing his second. Again, another long gulp and the glass was almost empty. He lit a cigarette, took a deep pull.

"Why aren't there any bottles behind the bar? I don't see one whisky bottle," Bud remarked.

"Wine and beer license. Not as expensive. Max started this place on a shoestring. A liquor license was out of his range," Dough told him.

"Didn't know there was difference. Don't think we have the same laws in Iowa," Bud said.

"This is Florida. It hasn't caught up to the twentieth century yet," Dough added. "By the way, there's a party at The Shack tonight. Why don't you make it over there and see if Max can help you? He'll be there, I'm sure."

"Whose party?" Bud asked, not wanting to be an interloper.

"Just a party. There's always a party somewhere on the beach."

"As long as I'm not odd man out. I just got here. Don't want to start off on the wrong foot."

"Just show up. The Shack's on the main drag in Dania. Stay on Seabreeze till you get to US 1, turn left, and it's down about two miles. You can't miss it." Dough finished his beer. Bev placed another before him. He finished it off in one gulp, put his cigarette out, and threw some coins on the counter.

"See you tonight," he said, disappearing into the failing sunlight.

Bud sipped his beer slowly. There was no way he could chug-a-lug the way Dough had.

"Want another?" said a voice from behind the bar.

Bud's reverie broken; standing in front of him was another beauty with dark brown hair about as old as Bud. Across her well-endowed T-shirt was written "Cass."

"Eh?" Bud said.

"Do you want another beer?"

"No. I'll finish this."

- 3 -

The door had been left open, letting the sea breeze blow away the rank odor of the bar. On the distant horizon, the tiny images of what appeared to be ships were silhouetted on the vast seascape. The beach with its pristine white sand and its surfeit of beautiful girls was inviting. Bud felt wide awake even though he hadn't slept in hours except for the snooze on the beach. *Ft. Lauderdale will rejuvenate me both mentally and emotionally*, he thought. He finished his beer and headed out.

"Hey, you forgot your butts," Cass called.

"They're not mine." He remembered Dough was smoking Marlboros. "They're Dough's. Hold them for him."

***

Jogging across A1A to the beach he stood on the sand breathing in the fresh salt air. There were a few late swimmers and sun worshippers. The sea breeze refreshed him. The rancid odor of the bar disappeared. It felt liberating to be on his own, and free of family restraints. He wasn't sure what the future held for him. Eventually, he'd continue his education. But major in what? Just a BA was not enough in this day and age. And what kind of career was out there for him? He had no idea.

Bev ran past him, dropping her towel, and diving into the breaking waves. She swam out a way with an elegant stroke, evidently a good swimmer. She began playing mermaid, diving and resurfacing.

"Did you find a place?" she yelled.

Maybe Dough was right. It wouldn't take that long, whatever that was. "Not yet. But I'm still hoping," he said, grinning pleasantly.

She looked like Amphitrite, wife of Poseidon, with her aquiline profile and long, blonde hair falling flat against her back. This was truly a goddess of the sea, Bud thought.

"Come on in," she called, disappearing under water, coming up at the water's edge a few feet from him.

"I'd rather watch you," he said.

"I do this every day. It's like putting on a new body after working all day at The Box."

How could she improve on what was perfect? She was backstroking away. He swept his T-shirt off and swam to her.

She greeted him with a playful, "Hello. How do you like Lauderdale?

"Haven't been here long enough to have an opinion. But it looks like it's going to be fun."

"Most people who come to Lauderdale are tourists. That's what I was eighteen months ago. Now I don't think I'll ever leave. This is paradise," she said, reaching out, drawing Bud near and effortlessly swinging around on his back, resting.

She wasn't sure about what was happening, but there was an immediate attraction. She felt it the moment he walked into The Box. It could have been the innocence that appeared on his face when asked for his ID. Or it could have been the way he didn't leer at her as others have done. Or try to hit on her thinking she was just a bartender grateful for the attention. She could feel how uncomfortable he was by her cheekiness. It was a first for her. Her reticence about dating since living in Lauderdale was legendary. The few guys she dated could be counted on one hand. She hadn't felt this attracted to someone in a long time. And that past, regretful relationship was something she never dwelt on. For now, she was content to see where this would lead.

Her body was warm against his. She wrapped her legs around his waist, feeling secure. Nothing was said, as they gently swayed with the rolling waves, letting whatever was happening continue. It was as if they conjoined, and both became one. It was unadulterated pleasure. He began to breaststroke with Bev lying prone on his back.

"You could become a lifeguard. It's not a bad job. And you can be on the beach all day. If you're going to stay here, you'll need a job. And guarding is about the only thing that makes you feel human when you have all this sun. It's better than sitting in an office all day. Or waiting on tables. Or pumping gas. You name it, beach patrol is better. From the way you so casually let me piggyback you, I'd say you're a good swimmer. You'd make a good guard."

"Sounds good. Who do I speak to?"

"Speak to Dough. He's the superintendent of guards."

She slid from his back and headed to shore. Bud watched her glide effortlessly through the water. She toweled dry, patting her body like a mother gently patting a baby.

"Here." She threw him her towel as he came out of the surf.

He dried himself as they walked up the beach.

"I live above The Box. Want to come up? There's some cold beer in the fridge."

He wasn't sure he hid his surprise when he said, "Sure."

She skipped across the street, her bikini hiding nothing from his imagination. She was perfectly proportioned. Tall, small backside, shapely legs, proud breasts, athletic body.

She closed the door on a studio apartment. The entire room was windowed overlooking A1A, the beach, and the ocean. Two single beds made up to look like couches were against one wall. End tables were on either end, with silly looking palm tree shaped lamps. A radio sat on one table playing "The Letter" by The Box Tops. A small alcove, separated by a small portable bar and two barstools, served as the kitchen. To the left of the front door was the bathroom, door partially open. The apartment was no bigger than an average living room, but because of the surrounding windows and unending vista, the impression was of something much larger. There was a light blue throw rug on the floor and white vertical blinds on the windows.

The Slow Wave

The apartment was spotless. Nothing was out of place. A few fashion magazines were on the small coffee table perfectly placed with an ash tray over to one side. A small bookcase made from wooden planks and building blocks was under another window. Paperbacks filled the shelves. *Sex and the Single Girl, The Group, Franny and Zooey, The Catcher in the Rye, Catch-22,* and *The Feminine Mystique* were among them.

"It's not a palace, but it's home. I need a shower. The salt drives me crazy. Make yourself comfortable. Beer's in the fridge."

She disappeared into the bathroom, leaving the door ajar. The shower went on. Bud took a Miller from the small fridge and settled himself on one of the couches.

He was intrigued by what was happening, and surprised it had happened so quickly. It was the first time a girl had taken the initiative. That had never happened before. He was both delighted and apprehensive. On the other hand, he could be completely mistaken. Maybe she was just being polite, helping a stranger find his footing. But then again, he hoped that whatever it was would materialize into something more substantial. He felt it when they were swimming. Something special had happened.

"If you're going to The Shack tonight, I'll go with you, if that's okay?" she yelled from the shower.

"Okay."

"What did you say?" she yelled.

"I said, okay."

"I can't hear you."

He crossed the room. "I said, it's okay. Did you hear me that time?"

"Loud and clear. Give me one of those towels, will you?" Her hand popped out from behind the shower curtain. The water stopped. The towel disappeared into the shower. The shower curtain was flung to one side.

Expecting to see her in the flesh, Bud was surprised to see that the towel was expertly wrapped around her and tied in front.

"Your turn," she said stepping past him into the living room.

"I left my clothes in the car. All I have is this bathing suit and T-shirt."

"You don't need anything else."

"Doesn't it get cold here at night?"

"If you think eighty degrees is cold, then you need clothes. Otherwise, you're dressed for almost anything in Ft. Lauderdale. This is a one-horse town, catering only to the college crowd. No need to dress for anything here."

He got out of his swim trunks, ducked under the shower, and adjusted the water level, letting the cascading water soothe him. In less than five hours he had met one of the most attractive girls he'd ever seen, was taking a shower in her apartment, and taking her out that night. This was quite a change from what he was accustomed to back home. He turned the shower off, toweled dry, and put his swim trunks back on.

Bev was lying on the couch. Eyes closed, listening to the music pumping out of the radio. His beer had been moved onto a bamboo coaster on the small coffee table.

"How do you feel?" she asked, not opening her eyes.

"Great."

He reached for his beer and sat beside her, beer in hand. This lovely creature was lying here. What was he going to do? If he kissed her, would that break the spell? Or would she invite more? He gently touched her face, her lidded eyes, her Grecian nose, and sensual lips. She didn't stir but breathed deeply. He slowly bent to kiss her.

Bev drew him close and kissed him back. Her arms wound around him, her hands into his hair, bringing him to arousal. Slowly, he maneuvered his body to lay against her. Their lips never parted as he continued to move in rhythm to her body. He felt as though he had known this body all his life.

He undid her towel, feeling the firmness of her breasts. His mouth reached for the fruit and drank of its pleasure. He slid his swimming trunks from his body. They lay naked against one another, muted sounds of lovemaking. He drew up on his hands, looking into her face for the same pleasure he was having. Her eyes were closed, a faint smile of pleasure on her lips, purring like a Cheshire cat. He began kissing her all over, wanting to explore every inch of this new country. She returned his passion with muted delight.

She maneuvered him in position to enter her. He declined, not wanting to end this wonderful sensation. He could wait, knowing that anything less than abstention would be final. He moved to taste the honey of her cone. His insides cried out for release. Her purrs became moans. Both wanted each other. Both could not wait any longer. She drew his head up and kissed him passionately. Exquisite pain shot threw them both.

"Please ... please ..." she whispered and kissed him harder.

He felt the warmth of her. Excitement and pleasure swept through him in torrents of passion.

She cried out as she climaxed in a frenzy of uncontrollable emotion. He joined her in painful pleasure.

They lay side by side, exhausted, breathing in unison. What pleasure. What joy. This was lovemaking Bud had never experienced. They lay silent and fell into a deep peaceful sleep together.

- 4 -

A ray of sun hit Bud across the eyes, stirring him awake from a deep sleep. His hand reached out. Nothing. He sat up, suddenly wide awake. That beautiful body, the enchantress of the night before had vanished. He didn't see her in the apartment. Was what happened a dream? Did he really meet a beautiful, blonde Venus? And did he make love to her?

He searched for his bathing suit and T-shirt. They also had vanished. His movements were slow, sleep still trying to take precedence. He shielded his eyes from the bright morning glare. In the bathroom a note pasted on the mirror: "At work. See you later, Bev" scrolled in perfect flourishing letters. Below the writing was a drawing of his swimsuit and T-shirt with a bubble, like in a comic book, saying, "Look behind you." The message looked more like a magazine advert. He smiled knowing that last night was not a dream. On the shower curtain rod behind him hung his bathing suit and T-shirt.

He hung them on the towel rack, jumped in the shower, and adjusted the water to his liking. Sleep was washed away in a cascading torrent of liquid life. He toweled dry, wrapped it around his waist, and went looking for his morning elixir. A half jar of instant Maxwell House coffee stood on the shelf in the kitchen. He filled a small pot with water and put it on the stove, then spooned a heaping spoonful of granules into a cup. Standing by the window, he looked out over the sun-drenched beach. Sunbathers were there. Scotty, the lifeguard he met yesterday in The Box was at the lifeguard stand talking to other guards. The surf was calm. Music from The Box drifted up. "Ode to Billy Joe" lamented a tragedy.

Bev was sitting behind the bar with a cigarette in the ashtray beside her when Bud came in. A dark-haired girl was leaning against the jukebox. No one else was there. Bev smiled warmly.

"Sleep well?" she asked.

"Great."

"I washed your trunks and T-shirt when I got up."

"Thanks, but you didn't have to."

He looked into her chocolate-brown eyes trying to find an answer to last night's exhilarating pleasure. Those clear and bright eyes were holding no untoward secrets. She leaned over and kissed him gently on the lips and he knew he had satisfied her in more ways than carnal.

"I moved your car, so you wouldn't get a ticket. It's out back."

"That car needs a hose."

"There's one in back. Max won't mind."

"What time is it?" He pointed to his wrist, which was bare. "Left my watch in the car."

"Twelve thirty."

"I slept for eighteen hours! I can't believe it. I know I needed sleep, but that's overdoing it."

"I didn't want to wake you. You looked so peaceful lying there."

"What time do you start?"

"Eleven. But I'm an early riser. I made so much noise I thought I'd wake you. You were out for the count."

"I have to find a place. See you later."

"No, you don't," she said. Her ingenuous look confirmed that she was serious.

He was about to say thank you, but she put her finger on his lips to silence him.

"No need," she said.

He backed out of The Box, keeping his eyes on her, pleased and pleasantly surprised.

***

He moved his few belongings into the apartment. It took half an hour to wash the MG and bring it back to life. It looked like new when he finished. He checked the motor, oil, and spark plugs, to make sure everything was secure after the long drive. Water and brake fluid looked okay. He took the tonneau cover out, wiped the dirt from the creases, and snapped it in place. He hadn't had this on in months. Iowa was not the place for a convertible. The top had been up since he bought it.

When he was finished with the car, he went back to the bar for a beer. He was parched after cleaning the car. Bev set a beer before him.

"I'm off at five. Everyone goes to Omar's on Sunday. It's like a jam session. You can meet the beach crowd," Bev said.

"Sounds good. Back after a swim," he said, and kissed her lightly on the lips. He headed for the surf across A1A.

He had to hop quickly across the burning sand. He stood looking out over the ocean, thinking how fortunate he was. In his wildest dreams he had not thought that he would meet someone like Bev. Or if he did, not so quickly. Basically, he wanted only a respite from the turmoil he was escaping from. No more arguments with his father. No more tiptoeing through life to make his father happy, if he was ever happy. Nothing he did seemed to satisfy his dad. That wouldn't be a problem anymore. He was on his own now.

A few bathers were in the surf. Children, watched by their parents, played in the shallows. Down the beach, Bud saw the dark-haired girl who was in The Box earlier. She was standing knee deep in the surf, splashing herself gently. Her light cotton dress tight against her body. He wasn't sure, but she looked pregnant. She continued splashing herself with water then lazily started off down the beach, kicking at the water as she did.

Bud walked into the surf, surprised at how small the waves were and how tepid the water was. The ocean should have big waves and surfboarders. These calm waters reminded him of the lake back home. Ft. Lauderdale was evidently not a surfer's paradise.

After a swim, he lay on the beach to continue the suntan that already started. His pallor was in sharp contrast to everyone he'd seen. He tanned fast. In a few short days he would look like the Coppertone baby. He had burned badly one time at the lake a few summers ago when he had fallen asleep, and no one woke him for five hours. He wouldn't let that happen here. He had already been lucky when Dough woke him yesterday.

Propped up on his elbows he surveyed his new surroundings. How long would he stay? Should he go back to college? What kind of job should he get? Should he write Sheila? Should he write home? Maybe a postcard? These were all questions for which he had no answers. Or maybe he didn't want to find answers? He was independent now. He wanted to enjoy it. No explanations. No excuses. That was his life before he left home. Right now, he wanted distance from his past. An unknown and exciting future was before him. The weather-beaten clock above one of the stores along A1A read four fifteen. He had time for more sun.

"Hey, you," a voice called.

A lifeguard about his age was tossing a football into the air. "We need one more. How about it?"

"Sure."

Eleven lifeguards were waiting. Insignias with Ft. Lauderdale Beach Patrol were on all their swimsuits. They were brown as ebony, over six feet tall, solidly built, and all in the late twenties to early thirties. Their faces wore the ravages of hard living.

"Name's Johnny," he said.

"Bud."

"You play on Mike's side. That evens it up," Johnny told him.

"We're down the other end," Mike said.

One by one they called out their names, Jake, Windy, Alex, and Jimmy. Bud introduced himself.

The ball spiraled through the air. Mike caught it and charged, his teammates running interference. This was serious playing. NFL without pads. Johnny hit the sand from a block by one of his opponents. Others went flying. Mike among them. The game progressed at a fast pace. This was very rough two-hand touch like Bud had not played before, each play professionally executed. Bud felt pain from being blocked. Passes were thrown for most plays, but that didn't prevent body contact. As tactile as it was, there were no arguments. No contentious words. They were all friends, and all in excellent condition. But for whatever reason they played like adversaries. The frustration and disappointment of not achieving their initial goals earlier in life came out in a barbarous game of touch football. Bud fit right in. Within minutes, he was hitting and blocking as hard and forceful as the others. Every block he threw was a wish fulfilment of retaliation. Bud had no idea how much time had passed. When shadows started to fall across the sand, he noticed that the clock across A1A read 5:45. He was late.

"I have to go," he called to Mike.

Mike waved him off, "See you around."

Bud headed for The Box. His place was taken by another guard who had been watching from the sidelines.

The Box was full. Bev wasn't there. Cass, the girl who had replaced Bev yesterday, was pulling beer.

"Have you seen Bev?" Bud asked.

"She's off," Cass replied.

"Thanks."

He ran up the stairs to the apartment. The door was open, and Bev was at the window watching the football game.

"You're not bad," she said when he came through the door.

He kissed her. "Thank you," he said.

"I've been watching. Didn't want to bother you." She gave him a bottle of Miller.

"Let me wash the sand off," he said, "Then we can go to …"

"Omar's." Bev finished his sentence.

He was splashing Old Spice on his face when Bev came to the bathroom door. There was an enigmatic smile on her lips, as if she knew what was going to happen. He reached for her. She took his hand, pulled him toward her, hugging him passionately.

He was totally at ease with this beautiful creature.

"You smell good," she whispered and drew his lips to hers.

They kissed.

- 5 -

Lying in each other's arms, he wanted to say something endearing but couldn't find the words without thinking how banal they might sound. He was more than happy but didn't think he could express it fittingly, so he chose to remain silent. Better to go with the flow than appear dumb. How long would this sublime happiness last? He erased the pessimistic thought immediately.

He came to Ft. Lauderdale to get away from forced responsibilities, responsibilities thrust upon him by his micromanaging father. It was as though his father had never left the Army. He wore his hair Army style: short back and sides. The house was uninviting in its sterile perfection. Nothing was out of place. He made sure to let Bud and his mother know what was expected of them. Bud's room was always singled out as not being perfect, not tidy. When Bud told him he wasn't that interested in joining his father's CPA firm, things got even worse. He couldn't convince his father that he wasn't wasting his life not choosing a CPA career. Bud had no desire to sit behind a desk all his life going over numbers. He was frustrated and angry he couldn't make his father understand he had time before he made a life choice. His father was paying his college tuition and felt his son was obligated to him. Bud had no career choice in mind, but CPA was high on the list of "no-nos." His main interest, athletics, which came naturally, was out also. A damaged knee in a football game saw to that. Fortunately, it kept him out of the Army also—4-F was his classification, meaning someone unfit for military service. His father wasn't pleased that he wouldn't serve his country like he did. The pressure on him was so great that he tried twice, unsuccessfully, to enlist in the Army Air Corps and the National Guard. If the war had to be used for something, getting him away from home was it. Many of his friends unfortunately embarked on that one-way journey to Nam. He knew how lucky he was.

Then there was Sheila, but he didn't want to think about her. He didn't need the guilt. He knew if he thought about her, he'd feel nothing but guilt. Three years going together was tantamount to marriage where he came from. He didn't want that responsibility either.

Bud was the first man Sheila had slept with. He felt guilty about that and continued going out with her. In time the guilt disappeared, replaced by convenience and friendship. Convenient because he didn't have to hunt around for dates, and friendship because they were friends. But not in love. Sheila brought up the subject of marriage indirectly: so and so were getting married; so and so were already having babies. Jokes about making their own baby.

There was a more germane reason for him leaving. He didn't want to stay in Ames, Iowa. He wanted to experience the world, life, travel—all the things he felt were exciting. Being stuck in a small midwestern town wasn't what he wanted. There was so much of the world to experience. Staying in Ames was not it.

To earn enough money to buy the MGB, his first step on the way out, he took a job at his uncle's dry-cleaning store. He was fortunate in buying the MG. A foreign student at the college was selling it but could not find any buyers. Ames was not a sports car community, and other students weren't interested. The MGB was left at the local car dealership, on consignment, where it gathered dust. To get rid of it, the dealership made a deal with Bud under the asking price to get it off his lot. Bud saved every penny he made working for his uncle to buy it. When his uncle found out what he was working so hard for, he loaned him the remaining balance. Both agreeing to keep it a secret from his father. His uncle Pete knew how pigheaded his brother could be. Transportation would set Bud free.

His buddies had talked a lot of about Ft. Lauderdale. Some had even taken Spring Break there. It was the most swinging place there was, a modern-day Sodom and Gomorrah. Beautiful nubile bodies were everywhere. The place was full of them. It was obvious why college students were attracted to Ft. Lauderdale; it was cheap, cheerful, and brought together coeds and frats with no supervision other than their morals. When he decided to leave, Ft. Lauderdale was his choice.

"Why so quiet?" Bev asked.

"Thinking."

"About what?"

"Nothing important," he said.

Bev looked at him skeptically.

"I mean it. I wasn't thinking about anything important," he continued.

"Okay. If you say so," Bev said. "Let's go to Omar's," she whispered.

"Okay."

She kissed him.

***

Omar's was packed. There was a line to get in. The guard at the door waved Bev in the moment he saw her.

The music was deafening, conversation impossible. The five-piece combo had the amps revved up maximum. A banner above said, "The Lost Weekends." People were shoulder to shoulder. Not an inch of space was visible. Bud and Bev nudged their way through to a table where some of the football players from the beach were. Windy, Jake, Alex and four bikini clad girls were sharing a pitcher of beer.

Bev introduced Bud. Judy, Ann, Betty, and Lin greeted him enthusiastically. There weren't enough chairs available for them.

Before Bud could locate another chair, Lin took his hand and led him to the dance floor. Bud eyed Bev in surprise. She smiled back, hunched her shoulders, as if to say, "Oh well."

The combo started playing "Funky Broadway." Lin shouted, "How long you been here?"

Bud shouted back, "Since yesterday."

"It'll grow on you in no time," she yelled over the music.

Within minutes, Bud's T-shirt was soaked. Sweat dripped off his forehead like water from a tap. It ran down his back in streams. Lin's hair was matted to her head, her bikini streaked wet, her body radiantly alive with sparkling droplets. Every move she made caused a flurry of droplets to fly in all directions. There were over thirty couples on the dance floor, which was built to accommodate no more than half that. No one seemed to mind. Lin led Bud back to the table when the music stopped. Another chair had been found. Lin sat Bud down on the chair and plopped herself on his lap. Then came another "Oh well" look from Bev. A waitress came by. Bud ordered two Millers.

"Who won?" he asked.

"Johnny's side, by one point," Jake yelled back.

The music started up again and everyone took off for the dance floor.

Bev was gyrating to the music like a professional go-go dancer. It pleased Bud that they were together. The music stopped, the lead singer announced a short break, and everyone returned to the table. The jukebox went on immediately. He ordered another Miller.

"Why weren't you at Jim's party last night, Bev?" Betty asked.

"Fell asleep," Bev answered.

Small knowing smiles appeared on Betty and Lin's face. They knew that excuse was weak. They also knew that Bev and Bud were more than likely fucking.

"Everyone's invited to The Shack later. Bob is buying the first round in honor of his new bar. He's built The Shack to his specific specifications, and one of his demands is that everyone who comes will have to carve their name in the bar to celebrate and for posterity," Judy said.

"Sounds good. We'll be there," came the response in unison from all at the table.

The unrestraint these people lived was palpable. They didn't seem to have any worries, any inhibitions, or any opinions. Everything was unrestricted. Jake collected contributions for a pitcher of beer and handed the money to the waitress, who then filled all the glasses, draining the pitcher.

Windy called out over the din of the bar, "I'm going broke. With all the drinking we're doing, I won't have any money to pay my alimony this month."

"Don't drink that much then," Bob shouted back.

The table was convulsed in laughter.

"That'll be the day," Betty said. "A day without drinking doesn't exist in this crowd."

"We can give it a try," Lin said.

"Let us know when," Judy responded. "I'll make sure I'm not here."

More laughter.

"Okay, okay. Enough," Windy added. "I'll just abstain for a few days. That'll save me a bundle."

The music started and everyone headed back to the dance floor.

"Is it like this all the time?" Bud shouted into Bev's ear.

"Only during the off-season. In the winter and spring when the tourists and college kids come, we're too busy. It's our way of letting off steam."

"I can see how it would be easy to get accustomed to."

"How right you are."

The group stayed at Omar's for the next two hours, then agreed to meet up later that night at The Shack. Bev, Bud, and Windy headed for The Sand Box.

"How long you been a guard?" Bud asked Windy.

"On and off for ten years. Came here after college one summer and took the test. I've been here ever since," Windy told him.

"I think I'll give it a whirl. I was a guard up home every summer."

"It's not a hard test. The only thing you have to really know are the breaks and holds. They're a little different than ones you use in a swimming pool, but they're easy to learn. Dough taught me in less than an hour."

The setting sun cast luminous shadows across the beach, adding a fantasy motif to the mist rolling in from the surf, causing the cars moving on the A1A to look like surrealistic prehistoric insects weaving through it.

Bev stopped at a leather goods shop. Thongs, wooden necklaces, belts, and handbags decorated the window. Windy continued on alone.

"Nice stuff," Bud said.

"I'd like to get that belt," Bev remarked.

Maybe he could get it as a present? Then he remembered, solvency wasn't his strong point right now.

The Sand Box was loud, activity frantic. The other guards from the football game were there. Bud greeted Johnny and Jimmy and their dates, who were the two girls Bud had seen when he first arrived. Marge and Delores were tall and as beautiful as professional models.

Dough was at the end of the bar. Bud led Bev through the crowd.

"Didn't see you at The Shack," Dough said.

"We got detained," Bev answered.

Dough arched an eyebrow, smiled knowingly. No need to ask his next question. He lifted his glass from the five empty already there in a mock toast, his smile becoming broader. Cass brought up beers for all of them.

"Windy suggested I ask you what's the chance of taking the lifeguard test?" Bud said to Dough.

There was a slight pause before Dough answered. He wasn't enthusiastic about the suggestion for reasons of his own. In fact, he wished the kid hadn't asked him. "Sure. Go to City Hall, fill out an application, and see what Cummins says. If he needs anyone, he'll okay a test. If not, you'd be better off going back home," Dough said curtly.

He was a little taken aback by the terse response and more so by the suggestion to go back home. There was definitely an edge to it. He wondered, *Why?*

"Thanks. I'll do it first thing tomorrow," Bud said.

Dough fixed him with a steely look, grabbed his beer and finished it off in one long gulp, threw some coins on the counter, and left.

***

Later, driving through Dania, on their way to The Shack, Bev pointed out the Four O'clock Club, where you could get a drink after closing hours and where the most obnoxious older people hung out. The one time she'd been there, a fight broke out between two women. None of the beach crowd went there.

Bud suddenly felt the atmosphere change. He didn't know how or where it came from, but there was a change. An eerie silence pervaded the area. Even the air smelled different. There was no salt air blowing or sea breeze. The streets were deserted. The houses and antique store fronts ramshackled. Stores were dark and ghostly. Aged signs proclaiming "Antiques" appeared in most of the darkened windows, his headlights lighting up their signage. It was as if the distant past of antiques hovering in the windows sent out unknown histories of peril and doom. Dark shadows from antique items—carved horses, dogs, bears, and the odd wooden Indian left on the street—followed him as he drove, their glass eyes never leaving him. A sudden anxiety came over him. Bev seemed to tense up. This was Dickens's "Bleak House" writ large, a veritable Madam Tussauds on a spooky, darkened highway. Doom hovered over everything.

As suddenly as it began it ended. The lights up ahead breaking the gothic spell they had just driven through.

"There it is," Bev said, pointing to a clapboard, single-story building looking as if a strong wind could blow it over. A large lopsided neon sign hung over the entrance that read, "The Shack." It lit up the entire area, bringing life back after the depressing few miles of Dania's antique roadshow. He parked on the grass along with cars already there.

"Doesn't look like much," he said.

"Bob's fixing it up. He got it cheap."

"I bet," Bud said.

Everyone from The Box was there. Bob was behind the bar pulling beer from an antique tap. He was an ex-lifeguard a few years older than Dough, weather-beaten but still in good shape. He decided to give up being a beach bum and try becoming a businessman. In contrast to the other beer bars on the beach, Bob had opted for a full liquor license, with beer, wine, and spirits. He'd invested everything he had buying The Shack. He sold his dilapidated house in Ft. Lauderdale and lived in the back of his investment. There was no Mrs. Bob. That had ended years ago. A narrow wood railing separated the room, half acting as a seat for those not at the bar. The other half of the bar was a restaurant, not utilized yet. The kitchen still had to be installed.

"Hey, what took you so long?" Johnny said from the end of the bar and waved them over. "Bud, I want you to meet the owner of the only antique bar in South Florida."

Bob laughed a hearty belly laugh and put three beers in front of them. Bud took a closer inspection of The Shack.

Liquor bottles sat on wooden shelves secured to the wall behind the bar. An assortment of movie star photos and film posters were tacked to the walls forming a huge collage. The walls were wood paneling with French windows leading to a patio. A straight back wooden chair and toilet seat hung from the rafters adding nothing to the elegance. There were a few small round tables and chairs on the other side of the divider. Two objects were incongruous: the cigarette machine and jukebox, modern misfits in a junkyard motif. The floor was rough cement.

Bev was listening to Judy who was not too happy how things were going at the car rental company where she worked. She was having problems keeping her boss away. Bev suggested she leave, get another job.

"What would I do?" Judy asked plaintively.

"I don't know. But there must be something out there."

"That's exactly what I mean. Uncertainty. I work from eight to three thirty. I don't take a lunch break, so I have the rest of the day to lie on the beach. Where else could I get a better deal than that?"

Bev had no answer for her. She was basically doing the same thing, doing something beneath her to lounge on the beach.

Bud remained silent, not sure any advice he would give would be helpful. After all, he was about to start a beach life with no future also. Who was he to give advice?

"Where you from?" Delores asked. She appeared from out of the crowd inches from Bud.

"Iowa, Ames."

"I've been to Des Moines. Ever been there?" She was closer than necessary, making Bud uneasy, especially since Bev was right there. He couldn't move. Sardines couldn't be packed tighter.

"For a football game."

"What made you come this far south."

"It was either California or here. I've never been to either place. Some college buddies always talked about Ft. Lauderdale. So, I came. I could always try California if I get bored here."

"Never happened. Bored doesn't happen in Lauderdale. What are you going to do?"

"Try out for lifeguard."

"Another one," she said, dispiritedly.

The sarcasm was evident. He was about to ask why when Bev linked her arm in his.

"Some people are going to The Chateau for breakfast," she said. "What do you say?"

"Sure. Why not?" he answered. "What's The Chateau?"

"A restaurant on top of The Tower office building overlooking all of Lauderdale. It's on A1A up the road from here. We always go there," Bev said.

"I have to be up at seven. And if I go, I know I won't get to bed before five," Delores said.

"What's happening at seven?" Bev asked.

"A job interview in Miami. Typing, shorthand. And I need some sleep."

"And if we don't get any," Marge broke in, "we might as well kiss the job goodbye.

Bud sensed that they could care less if they got the job. The indifference in what they said was evident.

The beers kept coming. The conversations bounced from one trivial subject to another without any constructive intent, mere verbiage to pass the time while beers disappeared.

Bob was telling them about the new combo he was trying out. He could not recall their name. But it didn't matter, they weren't staying. Even if they were good, they would not be hired. The weekend they played would be free. Then another combo would be hired, also free. The combos didn't mind the freebies; they needed experience.

All small bars in Ft. Lauderdale and surrounding tourist areas operated that way during the off season. Only the more substantial restaurants and hotels hired name performers all year round, mostly in Miami Beach. The Eden Roc, Fontainebleau, and Deauville were notable for this. Arthur Godfrey, Jackie Gleason, Frank Sinatra, and Perry Como were frequent headliners. On rare occasions, Sarah Vaughn, Eartha Kitt, Sammy Davis Jr., and Lena Horne appeared. Miami Beach was segregated and no matter how famous you were, Miami proper was off limits to Blacks—and Jews. Milton Berle loved coming to Miami Beach, but never ventured away from the nightspots. When one strolled the beach, you could see Jerry Lewis, Sid Caesar, or Groucho Marx sunbathing, but you never saw them strolling the streets of South Beach. It was mooted that Jack Benny and George Burns refused to go to Miami Beach. Ft. Lauderdale was a far cry from Miami Beach.

During the season, Bob would hire the combo who cost the least. He didn't use a professional entertainers' agency. He advertised in the various college papers. Combos came from all over the country.

The drinking started to affect Bud. He wasn't drunk but weaving. He had spoken to all the beach bums. One conversation intrigued him. It was with someone called Tony who had attached himself to the beach crowd.

Tony was from Boston. He was in Lauderdale just wasting time. He could afford it. His new sports car cost over eight thousand dollars and he'd put another few hundred into customizing it, down to a special steering wheel and stereo radio. Bud was envious. He wished he had lots of money. He'd be able to do anything he wanted. Tony talked incessantly about himself. He made no introduction of the beautiful coed sitting at his side. The few times he did talk to her were condescending and sarcastic. She just sat there smiling pleasantly. However, the look in her eyes said she was not happy, and more than likely, she would rather be any place other than where she was. She glanced stealthily at Tony tightening her lips in displeasure. *What a schmuck he was*, she was thinking and wished she had never accepted his suggestion to go to Miami with him. From now on, she would stay with her friends in Palm Beach. Any one of them was better than this egotist.

Bev sidled up to Bud, seeing how uncomfortable he was listening to Tony, and led him to the dance floor. His weaving was more pronounced. The combo was deafening. His clothes were soaked in sweat. His energy low. Any minute he knew he would drop.

"I think we should go," he said.

"Okay."

Bev led him outside, waving goodbye to their friends.

- 6 -

Bud uncoiled slowly, like a snake coming out of hibernation. There was a dull ache in his head. The shower was running. He ambled to the bathroom. Bev had woken him so he could go to City Hall and fill out the lifeguard application. He was sure he could have slept all day.

"Come in, we'll do this together," Bev said over the cascading water. It sounded like thunder. His head was pounding.

Life flowed back into his lifeless body under the water and Bev's ministrations.

"You're making this difficult," he said.

"No time for anything but a shower," she answered.

He reached out and drew her close, kissing her passionately. She broke from his embrace and jumped out of the shower.

"Later," she said.

Bud finished showering, shaved, wrapped a towel around his midsection, and came into the bright sunlit room almost fully conscious.

"Coffee?" Bev asked.

"Absolutely," he said.

She handed him a cup, the fuse to the rest of the day. Without it, he was certain to go out like a light bulb. He put on a pair of jeans and flip-flops and threw an Iowa State University T-shirt on. Bev had already made the beds and dressed, throwing on a pair of micro shorts and a The Sand Box T-shirt.

"What time is it?" he asked.

"Eleven thirty," she said.

"I thought you had to be at work at eleven."

"I'm off Monday," she answered, smiling.

"I wish I knew that a few minutes ago," he said. "What time did we leave The Shack?"

"Must have been around two or later."

"Did anyone carve their names on the bar?"

"You did. BUD in caps. You used a hammer and nail. It took you almost an hour." She pantomimed him slowly hitting a nail, then inspecting his work, like a gold prospector inspecting his pan, his nose inches from the bar, making sure it was perfect.

"I don't remember anything after the guy with the motorcycle came in."

Bev ran a brush through her hair, modeling her look in the full-length mirror on the back of the door. When she was satisfied, she closed the door behind them on the way out.

"Stay on Atlantic until you come to Sunrise. Turn left. You can't miss it."

The fresh air reawakened him fully. Bev's hair was windswept, her eyes half closed, filtering the morning sun. Bud was happy this beautiful creature had chosen him. His eyes were on the road. His thoughts on her. They pulled up at City Hall.

"I'll wait. It shouldn't take you long," Bev said.

City Hall architecture was institutionally bureaucratic, white brick, and glass. Functional. The inside was characterless, somber greys and blues and dull beige linoleum. A Black man was polishing the floor with an industrial polisher. Bud asked him for directions to the beach patrol office.

Fifteen minutes later, after filling out the application form and showing proof of age, Bud came back to the car smiling broadly and carrying an envelope. He had been lucky. At the suggestion of Commissioner Cummins a few months previous, a new city ordinance had been passed stating that the beach patrol was to be increased due to understaffing. Last season's shortage of lifeguards was proof of the necessity for more guards. Closing portions of the beach during high season was not an option any longer. The city council was fully aware that unsatisfied tourists would find alternative accommodations in other seaside resorts. The bottom line was obvious: lost tourists equaled lost income, something Ft. Lauderdale did not want. Consequently, Bud was the beneficiary of the recent change.

"Nothing to it. I just give this to Dough and take the test. Then I'm in," Bud said.

"Wonderful."

"Where to? It's your day." Bud said.

"Let's just go to the beach. I need a rest after last night. After you see Dough, we can go up the coast and watch the surfers," she said.

"Sounds good," he said.

***

Jimmy was on number 7 lifeguard stand across from The Box. Bud waved the test papers at him. Got a high sign in return. Marge and Delores were sunning themselves. Bev spread a beach towel on the hot sand, made herself comfortable, rubbed herself with lotion, and handed it to Bud.

"When's your test? "Marge asked.

"Wednesday," he said. "What about you? How'd your interview go?"

"We couldn't even move this morning. I knew I shouldn't have gone to The Chateau," she said.

There was no remorse in her voice. She blurted out her information as if she were an heiress with no financial worries.

"But we called. They said we could come down tomorrow," Marge said.

"I hope it works out," he said, earnestly.

"Bob needs a waitress. Why don't you ask him for the job?" Bev said.

"I couldn't take it. All those bikers hitting on you all the time. And those hours! I'm sure I'd go crazy after the first two days."

"Maybe you could split the hours with Delores?" Bev said.

"Good idea. We'll speak to Bob."

Bud settled himself on the blanket next to Bev and became one with the sun, which would be his life for the foreseeable future.

- 7 -

Jimmy called down from the stand. "Hey Bud, Dough's waiting for you. It's nearly five."

"Right," Bud said.

Dough's office was in the Johnny Weissmuller Swimming Pool complex, a block or two behind The Box. Bud was anticipating the challenge.

"Is Dough here?" he asked the guard at the entrance.

"At the end of the pool."

Dough was sitting on one of the benches surrounding the Olympic-size swimming pool under the shadow of the twenty-five-foot diving platform, shielding Dough from the burning rays of the sun.

"Thanks for seeing me," Bud said, coming up to him and handing him the test papers.

"No problemo. Do you remember the holds?"

"Yes."

"I'm sure you do. But the USLA must make sure beach guards know how to handle deep water victims. That's why I'm here to test you."

There was an authority about Dough that hadn't been there before. The more Dough explained, the more Bud felt he had never met this person before. The Dough of the night before certainly was not this commanding person explaining the life and death importance of being a Ft. Lauderdale lifeguard. He demonstrated some of the breaks dry, then asked Bud if they were what he had done in Ames. They were. Fifteen minutes later after doing a few other breaks dry, Dough asked, "Want to try a couple in the water?"

"Sure."

They jumped into the pool and swam to the middle, treading water as they talked.

"The most important element I'm concerned with, and the thing that can get you more points off your test, is an incorrect or loose hold. Let's go through one of the easiest, the tired swimmers carry."

Bud led him toward the side of the pool with the easiest hold in the lifeguard books. Then he did a cross chest carry and rear head hold release to cross chest. After a few more holds, all of which Bud knew, Dough was satisfied. He couldn't find fault with any of the holds. Bud wouldn't have anything to worry about.

Bud was pleased. Come midweek, he'd be a Ft. Lauderdale lifeguard.

"Let's go to The Box. I'll buy you a beer," Bud said.

"Sure. I have to drop this in the office," Dough said, holding up the test papers.

He led the way past the entrance to the museum of Olympic swimmers, and through the glass doors at the far end of the pool to his office.

It was a large airy room with leather furniture and a desk facing out across the pool.

Surfing pictures, group shots of lifeguards, and diplomas and certificates of accreditation hung on the walls. From anywhere in the office, the entire pool was in sight. Any swimmer thinking they weren't being observed, even though they couldn't see a lifeguard, would be wrong.

Dough sat at his desk, suddenly weary. He looked around the room vacant-eyed. After a few contemplative moments, he said, "I'm at the top. But the top of what?"

The irony, if there was any, escaped Bud. But the brevity of the statement held anxiety.

"There's nothing more I can do here. I'm at the top of the ladder and can't see anything in the future," Dough said.

He was staring at the wall of pictures but seeing nothing. As if speaking to himself, his rheumy eyes mirrored a history of despair. Bud became concerned. It was more dispiriting when he thought about the self-confident, caring teacher of a few minutes ago. What had brought on such a drastic change so quickly for no apparent reason?

Bud didn't know what to do. Should he say something to break the uneasy atmosphere? He felt awkward standing there. Shifting his weight from one foot to the other, he bumped the chair beside him, sending a high-screeching sound through the room.

Dough blinked, coming out of his trance-like state. Looking at Bud as if nothing had happened, and without preamble, he said, "Let's go to The Box."

"Right." Bud was sad but relieved that whatever it was that just happened was over. It was scary. The shock of seeing Dough in such a state gave him pause. For the life of him, he couldn't figure it out. One minute the guy was normal, easy going and professional. The next, he was withdrawn, maudlin, and definitely scary.

Cass, Bev's replacement, was behind the bar. She had a beer ready the moment she saw Dough and Bud.

"I'll go get Bev," Bud said.

She heard him come through the front door. "How did it go?" she called from bathroom as she toweled herself dry.

Lost in thought, he didn't hear. He stood at the window looking out over the sea, still thinking about the incident with Dough. When she tapped him on the shoulder, he turned to face her.

"Hi," she said. "You okay?"

"Yeah."

"How'd it go?"

"Okay. It went okay."

"Are you sure? You seem distant," she said.

"No. I'm okay. Let's go."

She was sure something had happened. The moment they entered The Box, his mood changed. A wide grin broke out on his face, and the tension eased.

Cass put another beer on the bar. Bev took a long pull eyeing Bud and Dough suspiciously.

"He'll pass," Dough said, interpreting her look as a question of Bud's fitness.

"Great. He needs a job," she said. *What the hell could have happened?* she asked herself.

Is that what he needs? A job with no future. Christ, what was wrong with him? Dough rebuked himself for being pessimistic. The kid is not going to be a lifeguard all his life. This is just a stop gap.

"Hey, where you been?" a voice broke in.

It was Tony, the loudmouth from The Shack. He was grinning like a Cheshire cat, carrying a mug of beer. Without being invited, he joined them, ignoring Bev and Dough.

"Bud, what did you think of that dog I had with me last night?"

Before Bud could answer, Tony continued, "I sent her home to the kennel before her friends could pick up the scent."

Dough quickly finished his beer, while eying Tony contemptuously. "I have to go. See you later." Then he left.

Bev leveled a criticizing look at Tony. She would have liked Dough to stay. She might have found out what had happened between Bud and him. Tony rattled on like a broken record. He had picked up the girl in Palm Beach, one of the local millionaire kids. She was twenty-one and screwed like a bunny.

He ordered two beers before Bud could say no. Bev tried finishing hers in two gulps, wanting to get away from this obnoxious person. Bud drained his glass and said, "We have to go." Then he took Bev by the arm and led her out.

"Don't do anything I wouldn't," Tony yelled at their backs.

"Who the hell was that?" Bev asked.

"I have no idea. He was at The Shack last night and just started talking to me."

"Lucky you."

"Yeah, right."

- 8 -

Jake, Windy, and Mike were sitting with Marge and Delores at Omar's when Bud and Bev came in. The drinking started. The night dragged on. By eleven thirty they were feeling no pain. Bud and Bev said good night. Marge and Delores said they were leaving also. They were going to Miami for the typing test tomorrow. As they left, Bud noticed a few rowdy guys who weren't part of the beach patrol. They were drunk, hanging onto the jukebox. They eyed each other on the way out.

Bud's liquid thoughts were on the last few days. It was weird. He felt as though he had been in Ft. Lauderdale for years. Home was a far-off place lost in memory. He lay in bed thinking about his meeting with Dough. What had caused Dough's momentary lapse of self-confidence? Bev was beside him. Her eyes held the question, *What are you thinking about?* Without saying a word, she brought her lips to his. They became one but fell asleep miles apart.

- 9 -

On the day of the lifeguard test, Bud was a little nervous. It was eleven in the morning, another bright sunny day in a cloudless sky. He was due at the pool by one o'clock. He got out of bed, showered, and dressed. With what had become his usual attire, T-shirt, and swim trucks, Bud entered The Box. He winked at Bev, who was behind the bar washing glasses. Off in the corner was the dark-haired pregnant girl he had seen before. She was holding an empty glass as if studying it. There was something enigmatic about her that made him stare. She returned his stare with a vacant gaze, got up, and left.

"Who is she?" he asked.

"Her name's Laura," Bev answered.

"She's pregnant, isn't she?"

"Yes."

"Who's the father?"

"I don't know. She hasn't told anyone."

"She looks lost."

"She's a Seminole. Everyone around here knows her. People tried to help her. But they gave up after a while. Frank and Rocky let her stay with them thinking she'd help around the house or something, but she didn't do anything but sleep. So, they asked her to leave."

"Maybe one of them …?"

"No. Not their type. Rocky wouldn't touch her. Frank is not too fond of her.

"Then why did they let her stay?"

"For all their bravado, they have big hearts. They thought if she had a place to stay, she'd find a job, get her own place. But she didn't."

"She's pregnant. How could they ignore that?"

"They tried. It didn't take. End of story."

Bud watched her as she splashed herself in the surf.

"Is that good for her?" he asked.

"I've told her not to a few times, but she still takes her bath like that every day."

"Bath?"

"Yes. She goes in for a while, splashes water all over herself, stands under the shower, then sits on the beach to dry. I don't think she has another dress. I've never seen her in anything but that red muumuu."

Bud shook his head in despair.

"I'm going to get some breakfast," he said, kissing her. "See you later."

"Try Mary's down the street. Cheap and cheerful."

He high-fived her and headed for Mary's.

A few days ago, Bud had walked into her life. His callowness attracted her immediately. When she overheard he was looking for a place to stay, her course was set. She knew she would sleep with him. She felt there was something special about him. He wasn't nihilistic like the others.

She usually took a nap after work, but when she saw Bud on the beach from her window, she made up her mind to make contact. And when he watched her in the water, she knew she would have him. She was glad she did. He was thoughtful, considerate, and an incredibly good lover.

In Chicago, where she worked for an advertising agency, she'd had an affair with one of her coworkers. When she found out he was married and that there was no future in their relationship, she left and came to Ft. Lauderdale. That was eighteen months ago. She was twenty-two with her whole life before her. Maybe Bud would be part of that life? She felt she was falling in love with him.

Bud finished breakfast with still half an hour to test time. He dodged the traffic on A1A and cooled his feet in the surf. Laura was lying on the beach, the sun beating down on her already darkened body. He said hello. She looked up, smiled. He sat beside her, not knowing what he would say or do.

"How do you feel?" he asked.

"Fine," she answered, her concentration on the far horizon.

He felt awkward not knowing how to continue. She must have felt his embarrassment. Getting up, she smiled and walked away. He watched as she disappeared down the beach, going nowhere.

The clock over the store across A1A told him he had fifteen minutes before his test. He headed for the Olympic swimming pool, arriving with two others who were taking the test. Johnny greeted them.

"Ready?" he asked.

They replied "yes" in unison. Bud knowingly winked.

"Dough'll be here in a minute," Johnny said. He checked their names off his clipboard.

Dough came out of his office carrying a clipboard. Scotty was with him.

Without preamble he outlined the test. "First part will be the 200 freestyle. It has to be completed in under four minutes." Dough was all business. Not a hint of the beach bum he was on his off hours. No friendly nepotism toward Bud.

"Start in the shallow end. No diving. Scotty will keep time. Johnny will verify," Dough finished.

They jumped in the water, which surprisingly was much colder than the ocean. Goose bumps began appearing.

"On your mark, get ready, go," Dough called out.

Pushing off the side of the pool, they fell into a rhythm that soon turned into a competition. Bud, knowing he had time, paced himself. He had done 200 in less than four minutes many times. He prided himself on being in good shape. He saw the feet of the other swimmers kicking in front of him as they pulled away from him. The first fifty meters were easy. On the second fifty, he noticed the feet of the swimmers starting to fall back. His pace remained the same, but his arms started to ache, and his legs hardened. On the third fifty, Bud lessened his pace, ignoring the pain that shot through him. His co-swimmers were falling behind, their arms hitting the water like giant fly swatters. Bud's arms started to feel as heavy as weights. He thought he was in better shape than this. Where was all this pain coming from?

One more lap he told himself. His mind started to wander. He saw himself driving to Ft. Lauderdale, in bed with Bev, swimming in the ocean, drinking at The Shack, at Omar's, in The Box. His whole life seemed to be flashing before him. He wasn't even aware that he was on the last lap. The pain was constant now. He didn't know how he was enduring it. Visions of summers in Ames clicked on and off. Sheila popped in and out of his vision. It was as though he was in a trance. He was washing his MG, showering with Bev, sitting on the beach talking to Laura, at The Shack drinking beer. His arm hit the end of the pool. It was over. He sank to the bottom of the pool, exhausted, then came up to get air.

"Good going," Johnny and Scotty were checking their stopwatches.

"Three minutes and thirty-two seconds. Great time, Bud," Johnny said.

"Take a rest," Scotty said. "We'll do the breaks and holds in fifteen."

Bud got out of the pool shaking himself loose. "I feel like one big knot," he said to Johnny.

His co-swimmers were doing the same.

"What was our time?" one of them said, twisting, turning, and bending to get the knots out.

"Three minutes and forty-five seconds," Scotty said.

All were thoroughly exhausted. Complicit smiles broke out between them, knowing they had passed the first part of the strenuous test.

"If there was one more lap," one of them was saying, "I'm sure I'd have dropped."

"Right you are," his companion agreed.

Bud tacitly agreed. He wasn't sure he could have gone another lap.

At the diving pool, Dough explained the next phase of the test, breaks, and carries. Scotty would work with Bud, he and Johnny with Bud's co-swimmers. He had already told Bud that he would not be able to do breaks and carries with him because of their friendship. "Bias," he'd said.

After their fifteen minute rest, they did the breaks and carries in less than half an hour. All that was remaining was the ocean save-and-rescue technique. They headed off to the beach. Each was given a torpedo can, which they had to use as a life preserver when they rescued a swimmer in distress. Johnny, Scotty, and Dough swam fifty meters out and shouted for help. All three raced into the water, carrying their torpedo cans; they swam as fast as they could to their victim, bringing him back with the correct hold, a cross-chest carry with can. On the beach they had to administer CPR; test time, within five minutes. It went off without a hitch. Remaining was a written test that they could take at the end of the week, and Dough's assessment of their ability. Then they would be lifeguards.

Everyone congratulated each other. Bud was invited to Pompano Beach by his two co-testers. That was their domicile. Cummins had scheduled them with his Ft. Lauderdale team since there were only two and the Pompano Beach test wasn't scheduled for weeks, and they were short of beach patrol. It was a favor reciprocated whenever the circumstances presented themselves.

Bud was dry heaving, nodding okay as they took off back to their car. Bud headed to the shower at the entrance to the beach to wash the saltwater off. His stomach ached, his arms hung like pendulums, and his legs were dead weights. He sat in a heap under the jet spray. Minutes later, he felt a little more human.

Dough, Johnny, and Scotty coaxed him up, almost carrying him to The Box. They ordered beers. Bev's grinning expression told him she was pleased. Bud had a job. Nothing more to worry about.

That night, Bud poured out all his happiness in lovemaking. They lay in each other's arms feeling their hearts beat. With each breath, her perfect breasts rose and fell. Their rhythmic breathing coincided. In the few days they had been together, he had learned about her sexual likes. A lingering kiss on the neck would bring her to ecstasy. She liked to roll up to him at night like a newborn calf snuggling up to its mother, nibbling his ear. She would tickle his toes with hers when she wanted to make love again. Light scratching on her back would put her to sleep after making love. The longer he spent with her, the more he enjoyed her. This lovely creature brought him happiness.

Making love to her was a pleasurable continuum. It would go on into the early hours, never ceasing to excite him, always satisfying each other. Nothing was verboten. They grew to know each other's bodies. They were the only ones in the world. Sheila never entered his thoughts.

She lit two cigarettes, handed him one. Cradled in his arms, she said, "I think I'm falling in love with you." He kissed her softly. The pleasure of his touch passed through her like a bolt of lightning. She felt as though she would levitate. There was no fatigue. They made love giving each other their souls.

- 10 -

The clock read 12:30. He couldn't remember falling asleep. Bev was at work. He drove to City Hall to take the final part of his lifeguard exam. It looked as though he would be in Ft. Lauderdale indefinitely. He let out a wild yell of happiness that stopped a fisherman from casting off. Bud waved. The fisherman shook his head, more than likely thinking it was another college kid who couldn't hold his liquor.

Beauty was all around him. Ft. Lauderdale looked like a luminous painting meant only for the cognoscenti of high art. Buildings of all colors and design, framed with a myriad of flowers from Lantana, buttercup, bougainvillea to periwinkle. All set against the statuesque palms lining every street he drove. He felt sorry for that ordinary person who could not elicit the aesthetic joy of this beauty. Where could he go with Bev to share the joy he was feeling? He would defer to her decision, being not acquainted with the beach. Together they would share his happiness.

The written test was over in twenty minutes. A few short pages of public relation questions, more like a job application than a quiz. The simplicity of it surprised him. The swimming test was obviously the major factor of being hired. If Dough felt the applicant wasn't qualified, no job would be offered. As soon as they found a place in the schedule he would be notified, Cummins told him.

He bounded into The Box grinning like a child who had found the cookie jar.

"You're looking at the new lifeguard from Ames," he said.

"Well, aren't we the happy one?" Bev said, smiling.

"After work I'm going to take you somewhere. I don't know where, but it will be a place only happy people go. Your choice."

"The beach. Not necessary to go anywhere else. We have everything we need to celebrate right here on the beach. I wish I could get off right now," she said.

"If you say so. I have to see Dough."

He bent over the bar, kissed Bev, and was gone. Bev was happy. It meant there would be stability in her life after the disaster of Chicago. Somewhere she thought there was a promising future with Bud.

***

"Where can I find Dough?" Bud asked Jake, who was on duty at the swimming pool.

"In the office."

"I passed," he said to Dough, who was sitting behind his desk.

"I know. Cummins just called. It shouldn't take long to find a place for you. With the season coming up, they have to have a full lifeguard quota. State law. No public beach area is to be unoccupied."

"I was surprised how easy it was. More of a public relation's exercise. A lot of yes and no questions about tourism."

"City Hall making sure we don't scare the money away," Dough said.

Dough explained what his duties would be and, ironically, how boring it would get. Sitting on the tower for hours on end could get boring, but there were ways to keep sane. "I always took walks every hour or two, up and down the beach. Spoke to people. Did a little public relations with the tourists. Got the cramps out. Stretch your legs. Being sedentary could tighten you up, and if there is an emergency, you could cramp up. So, keep active," Dough told him. "You'll find what works best for you."

Bud collected Bev from the bar, they changed into their bathing suits, and joined the regulars who spent their time lolling on the beach. Delores and Marge congratulated Bud on his job. Jake had spread the word. Bob was expecting all the beach bums at The Shack tonight to celebrate. First two beers free.

Betty and Lin showed up a short time later. Lin taught school. Betty was a bartender in Pompano Beach.

"How do you like teaching?" Bud asked.

"It's a job. I get the summers off. Teach only ten months a year. What more could I ask for?"

"Teaching kids is kind of hard, isn't it?" Bev asked.

"No. I make sure they do their work and don't go around fighting. It's easy. Elementary school is mostly babysitting," she said.

"Why become a teacher if that's all the importance it has for you?" Bud asked.

"I needed a job. Teaching is one of the easiest. Who wants to work in an office all day?"

Bud felt teachers should instill in children the excitement and joy of learning: the satisfaction of accumulating knowledge and the possibility of creating new knowledge. Not treat teaching like any manual labor job anyone could do. Some of his elementary school teachers were like that. Mrs. Roth, an oversized, overbearing disciplinarian who sat at her desk all day telling the class if they didn't learn it was their fault. Mr. Trask's only interest was birds; that's all he talked about. He was no more a math teacher than the man in the moon. School was a big disappointment for Bud. High school and college weren't much different. Even though he hadn't chosen a major, none of his teachers inspired him.

Jake came by, offering Betty and Lin a ride home. They all agreed to meet later at The Shack. Bud and Bev scampered across A1A, avoiding traffic, and ducked into The Box.

Some of the beach bums were there mixed in with the tourists. Bud ordered two beers. Tony was sitting at the bar.

"Going to The Shack tonight?" Tony asked Bud.

"Not sure. What about you?"

"Depends. I have a date with some broad from Miami," Tony answered with his usual sarcasm. "I heard you took the lifeguard test."

"I did. And passed. I hope to be assigned soon. It's a great job."

"You'll have your hands full with all the tail on the beach. I could become a lifeguard, but I don't need a job. More shekels than I know what to do with. Don't have to work ever."

Bud caught Bev's discerning look. He knew what she was thinking. Tony wouldn't last two weeks as a guard before he was either fired or knocked on his ass. His bullshitting was well known, and barely tolerated. As long as it didn't interfere with the beach crowd or cause them problems, Tony could say and do anything he wanted.

The girls he dated confirmed his arrogance. All he ever talked about was his money, his car and how being a rich Jew was such an asset in South Florida. He was disingenuous. He didn't believe that one bit. He only said it to the Jewish girls he dated. He was fortunate to look like a gentile. Light brown hair, bright blue eyes and six feet tall. The swarthy complexion most Jews were thought to have skipped a generation in his family. He took advantage of those assets whenever he ventured into Miami Beach or Palm Beach (bird dogging) looking for dates. He had another asset; his name. Tony Ellis. No semblance to being Jewish. The foresight of his grandfather on arriving at Ellis Island in the U.S. years ago to change Itzik Mastofsky to Joseph Ellis, knowing it would be beneficial in the business world of this new country he was immigrating to. Ironically, he was timid. The slightest indication that they wouldn't go to bed with him stopped him in his tracks. They found him harmless and tedious.

The jukebox screeched. Someone at the end of the bar yelled. Max was holding a young kid by the collar, ready to hit him with his huge fist. Scotty was trying to hold him back, with little success. Some of the beach crowd joined in, restraining Max. The young kid had made passes at Max's date after being told to cool it. Bud could see that the kid was drunk. He made a move in Max's direction. Bev grabbed his arm.

"Scotty can handle it," she said.

"It's okay," Bud said.

"You big fucking ape. I'll get you. You fucking bastard!" the kid yelled at Max.

The Slow Wave

Scotty went to the kid with a word of advice. "I'm telling you, for your own good, get the hell out of here before he rips you apart," he whispered.

"I'm not going anywhere, you goddamn cocksucker. You fucking lifeguards think you own the beach. You're just a bunch of dumb shits, that's all. Dumb fucking shits."

Bud brushed past the kid to make sure none of these hotheads got at each other, accidently bumping him. The kid let lose a punch catching Bud on the side of his head. Bud's instant reaction was a roundhouse right squarely on the kid's jaw, drawing blood. The kid went down not knowing what hit him. He was sitting on the floor holding his face in his hands, blood streaming through his fingers. One of his buddies dragged him away, cursing everyone in The Box.

Bud, Scotty, and Max went to the door, watching them kicking parking meters in frustrated anger as they disappeared down the street. Bud thought they looked familiar.

"I didn't mean to hit him. But …"

"It's okay," Scotty said.

"Thanks for the help. But you shouldn't have gotten involved," Max told Bud.

"I couldn't help it. Natural reaction. Don't know where it came from," Bud said.

"I hope that's the last we see of them. Those college kids go nuts when they drink too much," Scotty added.

"I won't let them in anymore. If we do see them again, anywhere, just ignore them," Max said.

Bev took Bud back to where they were sitting. Tony ordered beers. Bud emptied his glass, shaking from nerves.

"I'm glad that's over," Bud remarked.

"Let's go home," Bev told him.

"No, it's okay. The band's just warming up at Omar's."

"I don't feel like going."

"I'm telling you, it's okay. I'm fine."

She pleaded with him unsuccessfully. He gently led her outside.

"I'll see you later!" Tony yelled.

Bud waved him off. He and Bev walked to Omar's. When they got there, the two kids from The Box were standing there.

"Don't say anything," Bev whispered.

"I don't even see them," Bud responded.

The two kids stared maliciously at them as they disappeared into Omar's.

Omar's was packed. Bud and Bev fought their way through to the table where Mike, Jimmy, and Lin greeted them. The music was loud, the dancers thick on the floor. Bud ordered two Millers.

"I hear you're one of us," Jimmy said, smiling.

"Yeah. I'm now going to sit in the sun all day and count waves."

"Where are they going to put you?" Mike asked.

"Won't know for a couple of days."

"Probably down of South 3," Jimmy said.

"Where's that?" Bud asked.

"Tourist heaven. Nothing but little college girls from up North," Jimmy said.

Knowing nods passed between the lifeguards. Bev and Lin ignored them. They'd heard this dialogue before. Scotty, Jimmy, and Jake came in. They told everyone what had happened. Bud was embarrassed from all the attention. Secretly, he liked the acceptance it brought him though. They closed Omar's, celebrating right up to closing time. A light rain was falling as everyone said their goodnights. Bud and Bev walked home, letting the rain soak them.

***

Bud loafed on the beach as he waited to hear when he would be assigned. Windy, Jake, Jimmy, and Alex were on guard duty at their appointed stations. The same people came at the same time every day: Lin, noon after school; Betty, twelve thirty after she got up; Marge and Delores, who didn't pass the typing test, one o'clock. From the way they mentioned their failure, Bud knew they didn't care either.

The Slow Wave

"We didn't see you at The Shack last night," Betty said.

"Forgot about it," Bud answered.

"Yes, we heard. You're pretty good with your fists," Lin said.

"News travels fast, doesn't it?" Bud said.

"It's a small place, Lauderdale," Delores added.

They had seen Tony earlier that morning and he told them. Also, someone called The Shack after the fight and let Bob know. Bud was sure his one punch was the talk of the beach.

The day slipped by slowly; everyone was preoccupied with their own thoughts. The inertia of doing nothing all day, every day had permeated their lives. Daytime was a problem. Nothing to do except lie on the beach, which after months became boring. The night was their elixir. And the only time they were motivated. Their entire life revolved around the beach, The Box, Omar's, The Shack, and The Chateau. It never changed. Their indolence showed in their inertia.

Betty left for work. Lin got tired of sitting and wandered off up the beach. Delores had to go shopping. Bud and Marge were left.

"The day I got to Ft. Lauderdale, you were the first person I saw," Bud said.

"Really?"

"I was at a red light, and you and Delores walked by my MG."

She remained silent as though making up her mind about something while she stared at him intently. Firm body. Strong features. Typical college haircut: short on top and lean on the sides. Classic lifeguard.

"You walked by again not too long after. Dough saw me watching you."

"What did he say?"

"I can't remember," Bud lied.

She knew that wasn't the truth. The way he blushed when she asked was written all over his face. She'd been in Lauderdale long enough to know what all the guards thought about women. They were either doable or forgettable. She also knew she was doable. If the guy was pleasant and not part wolfman, she'd have a go. Nothing steady. But a one shot to satisfy her was all she required. She was pissed off that all the men she met since she started dating at the age of thirteen had that philosophy—one-night stands. She adopted that philosophy, and it suited her very well.

Marge said she'd had some decorating done on her apartment and wanted a man's opinion. If Bud was free he was invited. Bud agreed but said his knowledge of decorating was nil. She wasn't interested in Charles of the Ritz opinion, just a masculine comment would be sufficient.

Marge lived behind Mary's, a favorite of the beach crowd. Cheap and cheerful. The one-bedroom apartment was furnished in used furniture: a couch worn to the nub, an easy chair with its stuffing coming through, end tables and a coffee table without distinction except that they were old, vertical blinds that had seen better days. The bedroom had a queen-sized bed, covered in a multicolored duvet with a huge teddy bear resting on the pillow. The apartment and furnishings may have been old and worn, but spotless. Bud had seen sorority apartments at college. This was a major surprise.

"That rug is the only new item in the place. What do you think?" Marge said, pointing to a beige throw rug in the middle of the floor. There were dark splotches all over it, similar to dog shit. If she hadn't said it was new, he would have thought a dog had been at it. Also, the color was questionable. Light brown? He wasn't sure. The spots were darker than the main color, which is why Bud thought a dog had gotten to it. He didn't want to hurt her feelings. He ruminated a while, making sure he would be tactful.

"It's an interesting brown," was all he could come up with. It was inane, but he was at a loss for anything complimentary to say.

"Want a beer?" she asked, ignoring his remark.

He was glad to get away from the subject of the rug.

"Yes," he answered.

"I know it's a strange design, but I thought it would make the apartment warmer," she said.

Bud could still not bring himself to say anything. Strange design was being nice. More like putrid. To be blunt, it was repellent. He sat on the couch, picking up one of the fashion magazines on the coffee table to keep from appearing critical. He didn't want to continue discussing the rug, which he felt would be awkward. Marge brought him a can of Miller's and sat beside him.

"I just want a sip," she said, taking the can.

She drank slowly with caution and exactitude holding the can in both hands, almost caressing it. Bud could feel the sexual tension in the air. It was evident she was making a play for him.

"I have to change my bathing suit." She disappeared into the bedroom, leaving the door open.

Bud could see her every movement in the mirror and he kept his eyes on her, arousal beginning. She slipped out of her bathing suit. Her breasts were large and perfectly formed, standing proud. The nipples of baby pink stared at him invitingly. Her firm ass molded tight, Venus his only comparison. He sipped his beer, keeping his eyes on the reflection in the mirror. She posed, knowing he was looking. The angle of the mirror made certain of that. She waited for him to decide. She would have him even if it took ten minutes of standing there.

Bud felt his loins stiffen. The male ego being tempted had no adjudication to stop what it knew to be infidelity. He went to the door. She opened it before he got there. He could now see how genuinely beautiful her body was. She wrapped herself in his encircling arms.

Making love to her was over in minutes. No emotion. Just carnality. With nothing to say to each other, he made a facile excuse to leave. "I have to check the guard's schedule to see if I'm on it," he said. She did not try to stop him. She was brushing her hair when Delores came into the bedroom, said, "Hello," to both as if seeing both naked was as trivial as making a cup of coffee, and went back out into the kitchen. Bud put on his swimsuit and left without saying anything, glad to be free of the awkward situation.

He had never experienced such sexual informality. Fraternities and sororities were always cohabitating, but not with such casualness. Showing no emotion whatsoever, Marge finished brushing her hair and went to help Delores.

- 11 -

Bev was in the shower. Bud stuck his head in the bathroom and yelled, "Hello!"

"Hi," she called back, peeping her head out of the shower curtain and throwing him a kiss. She then came out drying her hair with one end of the towel, while the other end modestly hid her body. Before she could touch Bud, he was in the shower washing off the foreign body that he had used.

With a towel wrapped around him, he looked out the window at the vastness of the ocean, full of guilt.

"Want something to eat?" Bev asked.

"I'm going to take you out tonight," he said.

"It would be just as easy to fix something here."

"No. This is my treat."

"Okay. But you have to budget yourself. You won't be getting paid for two weeks after you start on the beach."

He was low on cash, but he could make it through the next few weeks if he didn't go around buying beer for all the beach bums.

"Nothing expensive, but let's go out," he said.

They drove to Pompano Beach, almost in silence, to a little seafood restaurant Bev knew. His conscience was on the edge. He was afraid to say anything, not sure he could control hidden emotions. To pacify the situation, he blurted out a banality he immediately regretted, "I'll help with the rent."

"Don't worry about it," she said.

"What do you mean, don't worry about it?"

"I have a job. You don't have anything to worry about."

"What do you mean, I don't have anything to worry about?" he said.

"I didn't mean anything."

"You must have meant something. The implication is obvious."

"It means, you don't have to start paying rent the moment you get paid, that's all," she said.

"You think I'd like letting you foot all the goddamn rent?"

"No, off course not. And let's stop arguing. It's not important."

"It's not important to you, but I feel like a leech not being able to contribute."

"Please, Bud, you're making it sound like I'm keeping you."

"Well, aren't you?"

The guilt he felt came out in anger against the one person who didn't deserve it.

She held back tears that could easily come. Bud's remark shocked her. She could think of nothing to say that would recapture their original happiness. She was also afraid to say anything that may lead to more contention.

The drive home was tense. The silence unbearable. The tension tangible.

He lay awake forcing himself not to touch the person who could alleviate his guilt. Bev wished he would make a move to break this barrier that had come between them for no apparent reason. It couldn't just be the mention of rent.

- 12 -

The letter requested he report to Mr. Cummins at the Parks Department for his assignment. A jolt of happiness shot through him stronger than when he received his draft deferment. He would have the money he desperately needed and the security he wanted. Arguments about money wouldn't happen again, but he knew that wasn't the real reason for his anger.

Bev was at work. He didn't stop to tell her about the letter. He couldn't muster up the courage. Guilt weighed heavily still.

Mr. Cummins welcomed him into the Beach Patrol. He handed him his gear, two red Ft. Lauderdale beach patrol swim trunks, a first aid kit, a torpedo-shaped life buoy, and the phone link to keep in touch with headquarters. He was responsible for all the gear.

His station was South 3, as Jake had said. It felt good finally doing something useful besides pathetically lying on the beach all day full of anxiety about his indiscretion. Somehow he would have to find a way to right the wrong.

It was early; no one was on the beach except for an elderly couple sitting in the shallows cooling themselves like giant hippopotamuses. The sturdy wooden lifeguard stand stood five to six feet off the sand on solid four by fours. It was painted stark white and had a sky-blue slanted roof, like a Swiss chalet, with a four- or five-foot overhang. Steps lead up to the lookout deck. The guard had the choice of sitting inside observing through the large open-air window or sunning himself on the small deck fronting the stand. There was a Ft. Lauderdale flag secured to the stand along with the Stars and Stripes. Bud made himself comfortable on the deck, full of self-confidence as though he'd been doing this for years. The overhang of the roof protected him from the ever-present sun. If it became too uncomfortable, he could go inside the stand. The morning dragged on. The inactivity caused his mind to wander.

- 13 -

"I'll race you," Sheila said, as she hit him on the head with her towel and took off for the water.

Bud jumped to his feet in pursuit. She was running along the lakefront staying clear of the water. Bud swept her up in his arms and carried her out into the lake.

"Don't drop me. I'll get my hair wet," she pleaded, clinging desperately to his neck.

"What were you saying about a race?"

"Please Bud, don't drop me. I just washed my hair."

"I thought you wanted to race."

"I was kidding."

"Okay, this time. But next time, in you go."

He put her down, holding her close, feeling the warmth of her body and the joy it gave him. College was a fertile territory. Coeds everywhere. Existential opportunity. Was it necessary to sleep with every possibility? Wasn't it better to be happy with what he had? He had Sheila and she made him happy, but he ached with curiosity. The prospect of being faithful was questionable. And what about after? He hadn't thought about the future. His friends seemed to know what they wanted and where they were headed, if the draft didn't get them first. Luckily, he didn't have to worry about that. He knew that he wasn't going to spend his life in Ames. He was going to experience the world outside the confines of this middle class existence, but his college buddies were already planning to settle down with a wife and starting a family. He could sense it in Sheila. It wasn't for him.

Sheila carefully swam away so as not to wet her hair. She was the perfect hometown girl, right out of a Norman Rockwell illustration, and Bud was the only person she would ever love. He was the first and would be the last. It was a youthful dream and she luxuriated in it. She had already asked Bud if they would marry. Reluctantly, he said yes, but she could tell it didn't come from the heart. She wasn't Donna Reed, he wasn't Jimmy Stewart, and this wasn't Bedford Falls. Although Ames wasn't that far removed from *It's a Wonderful Life*. She wished he could feel the same about her as she did about him. She was going to college because it was expected of her. She had no career in mind, except that of being Bud's wife and mother to his children. Her only self-indulgence was acting in the college theater program.

They had talked about the future. Bud's father wanted him in the business. It was secure. Bud wasn't interested. He didn't know what he wanted, but he sure as hell didn't want to sit in an office all day hunched over an adding machine. She had patience. Eventually he would decide. And she would agree to whatever his decision was.

"How do you like it?"

The voice brought him up short.

"Hey, Bud, how do you like it?" the voice asked again. Dough was standing at the bottom of the stand.

"How goes it?" Bud said.

"Are you okay? Didn't you hear me?" Dough said.

Bud jumped down, almost collapsing.

"Hey, take it easy. You should take a walk every now and then, you know, so your brain doesn't go to sleep," Dough advised.

"Right. Wasn't even aware of time."

"So, how do you like it?"

"So far the only thing I've done is daydream."

"You'll have a lot of time for that," Dough said.

"It's not bad. I'll get used to it."

"Yeah, you'll get used to it," Dough dryly observed.

Bud thought he heard a bit of cynicism, but he wasn't sure.

"It's time for lunch. We can eat at Mary's."

Bud was about to say he had other plans, when Dough said, "Let's go." He put up the "Guard off duty–swim at your own risk" sign.

They jumped into the Beach Patrol Jeep and took off up A1A. Dough used his CB radio to report Bud out at headquarters. He parked in front of The Box and headed for Mary's up the street. Bud saw Bev forlornly watching them. He followed Dough, knowing he was being foolish for not going in.

They ordered hamburgers and cokes. Dough read the *Miami Herald* sports page.

"What do you say we go into Miami and catch one of the Dolphins games?" Dough said.

"Sounds good. Any time you like. Just say the word."

"I have a season ticket. We could catch one this weekend. I know someone who can get me an extra ticket."

"I'm working Sunday."

"We can fix that. Leave it to me."

It was the first time Dough had showed favoritism toward any of the lifeguards under his management. He was good friends with all of them but had never favored one in particular.

Bud was surprised and wondered why. The first time he mentioned lifeguarding, Dough's demeanor changed right before him. He made it clear that it was a major responsibility. A person had to be certain lifeguarding was the life they really wanted. It was as though Dough was warning him while at the same time explaining, but now he was making an exception and for the busiest day of the week, a day Bud knew all guards had to work—especially new guards. He was grateful for the magnanimous gesture but also confused by it.

Lunch finished, Dough said he had to collect something at his office. He'd pick Bud up after and give him a lift back to his station.

Bev was talking to Max as he waited for Dough outside The Box. Max saw him and came out.

"Bev says you saw those guys again," Max said.

"Yeah. In front of Omar's.

"When those kids get drunk there's no telling what they'll do. Wait until you see them over Spring Break. They're nuts. Thousands come here from all over. They sleep on the beach, in their cars, anywhere they can. And they drink the town dry. That's where it got its name, Ft. Liquordale."

He looked at Bev. A strained smile appeared. He wished somehow that the sorrow he was feeling would be metaphysically transmitted to her. She must have read his mind. Her smile broadened. Her eyes brightened. Dough drove up and said hello to Max. Bud got in and Dough drove off.

He left Bud at the stand. It was one o'clock, four hours to go. Bud called headquarters and reported back. The guard off duty sign came down. He made himself comfortable on the stand.

The beach had filled with frisbee playing teenyboppers. He guessed them between fourteen to sixteen. They were very attractive in their bikinis. Their little firm bodies wiggling whenever they moved was exciting to watch. He was glad he was wearing sunglasses. And sitting down. He could watch them without notice. A half hour later he jumped off the stand to patrol along the surf.

"You're new," said a pretty, petite blonde teenybopper.

He'd read *Lolita* and here she was, with a Barbie girlfriend. Nabokov was prescient. She was no more than five feet tall, but her dimensions were twice as big as Bev's. Her bikini couldn't hold back the voluptuousness of her breasts as they pushed out over her top. She wasn't tan, but ebony. Her blue eyes pierced him like fluorescent bulbs.

"Yes, I am," Bud said.

"Where's Scotty?"

"He's down on South 6."

She leaned back on her elbows, which made her look even larger than she was. Bud moved away, loins reacting to Lolita. He heard her say to her Barbie girlfriend, "He's cute," then giggle as teenagers do when they know older men are watching them.

He patrolled the surf thinking over how he would explain to Bev why he had made an ass of himself.

- 14 -

"You're twenty-one without a job. Do you think I pick money off trees?" his father said, angrily.

"No," Bud said.

"Why don't you get a job then?"

Bud didn't answer. It was obvious to him why he didn't have a job. And to his father. Part-time jobs in Ames were few and far between. Most stores and businesses were mom and pop entities. It was also obvious that this was another excuse to criticize him.

"I said, why don't you get a job? That way you could help out around here and not be a leech. You just sit on your ass all day and loaf."

Bud moved his lips, but nothing came out.

"What did you say?" his father demanded.

"Nothing. But what kind of job could I get that wouldn't interfere with my studies?"

His father laughed so loud, he started to choke.

"Interfere with your studies! Are you serious? Studying what? I don't know why I'm sending you to college."

Bud didn't either. When the Army deferred him, he was sure his father wasn't happy about it. His father's service record was outstanding. He'd experienced all the exploits of being in the war. Coming home after the war displeased him. He should have stayed in, become a career man. He liked the discipline, the regimentation. He used his GI Bill to get his BA and then take the CPA examination. It was very much like the Army. Disciplined. Regimented. Numbers were a constant. But deep down he regretted not staying in the Army. Getting married and having a child did not fulfill him. He was a dispiriting man. He was also frustrated that Bud wasn't interested in being a CPA. If it was good enough for him, it should be good enough for his son. It had widened the gap between them.

"I'll make a deal with you," his father said. "You get a job. Just pay for the food you eat. That's all."

Bud hatefully stared him down. "I'll ask Uncle Pete," he said, thinking anything to stop this ongoing friction.

"Ha. Peter doesn't need any more help. His shop is a two-man operation," his father chortled and left the room.

His uncle said yes, knowing the reason. He didn't need anyone at the dry-cleaning shop, but he knew his hardnosed brother and what he could be like. Monday, Wednesday, Friday, and Saturday morning, before classes started, Bud took the truck and delivered dry cleaning. And every week he gave his mother five dollars toward the food, which she reluctantly accepted. Unbeknownst to Bud or her husband, she put it away for Bud, knowing someday it would be useful for him. His father gloated. Bud hated every minute he had to endure his father's contentiousness, but he was saving also. Between tips and his salary, he would have enough by the end of summer to buy the MG he'd seen. He'd already put down a minimal payment. He'd known the owner of the dealership all his life. They had struck a deal. No one in Ames, college kids included, would buy such an outlandish car. Bud would no longer be subjected to his father's sarcasm when he asked to use the car. With his own car, he would be independent. Every time he thought of why he was working and what he'd been accused of, it made him tense.

***

Bud had walked to the far end of the beach where sand met private property, then started back. The phone was ringing. He sprinted back to the stand.

"Turner, South 3," he said, out of breath.

"Cummins, here. Turner. How's it going?"

"Okay, Mr. Cummins. It's quiet. Nothing to report."

"Be sure to collect your phone link. Most new guards forget them," he said, with a chuckle.

"No sir, I won't forget it. I'll make sure I have everything."

"Dough tells me you need Sunday off. It's okay with me. Johnny will replace you. You can make up the day later in the season," Mr. Cummins said.

"Thank you, Mr. Cummins." He hung up, wondering what Dough had told him.

He put all his gear in the MG. Looking out over the beach one last time, savoring the new position he had. From now on he would have security, the beach. The little blonde Lolita was looking at him. He threw her a fast Army salute, mouthing "goodbye." She waved back, keeping her eyes on him even as he drove off.

Anxiety made Bud approach the apartment slowly. He needed more time to think. If Bev were there, what would he do? How would he handle the situation? What could he say? How do you justify infidelity? He opened the door. The shower was running. He lay on the couch staring up at the ceiling. The cracks reminded him of lines on a road map. The shower stopped. He tensed, not knowing what to expect. Bev came out, one towel wrapped around her, another around her wet hair.

"How was your first day?" she asked without any trace of anxiety.

Go to her before you make it worse, he told himself. Bev stood drying herself, without any inhibition.

"Max said he really appreciated what you did," she said.

It was as though she was gliding across the floor. A vision coming to life. Beauty in motion. She bent down, the towel fell away, and she kissed him on the lips. He wound his arms around her and brought her down to lie beside him.

"I'm sorry," he whispered. "Sometimes I'm a total ass."

"I understand," she said.

Bud was relieved that he would not have to explain what had happened. He wasn't aware that she knew something had happened, and eventually she would find out. For now, she would appease the situation. From now on, he would be celibate and not let his prick take precedent over fidelity.

Their eyes met. Forgiveness in one. Regret in the other. He was thankful he wouldn't have to say anything. Lie more than likely. How could he tell his lover he had been unfaithful and expect forgiveness? Instead, he poured out his self-reproach in gentle love making trying to vanquish the tension and anxiety.

- 15 -

The Shack was crowded. All the beach bums were there, mingling with tourists. Beer came over the bar faster than Bob could pull it from the tap. A light rain was falling making it humid and uncomfortable. People were drenched in sweat. Bud and Bev were never without a beer. When one finished, someone would replace it. Between Dough, Johnny, Windy, Jake, and Max, Bud and Bev never had to pay for a drink. His vision became fuzzy. His stance unsteady. His senses dulled. His body uncoordinated. The music ear shattering. Everything moving in slow motion. Nothing in focus. Bud was certain something was wrong with his eyes.

"Let's dance," Bev said, pulling him onto the dance floor. Bud felt as though he were floating high above the earth. In no condition to move much less dance.

The music stopped the moment they joined the other dancers. Bev led him back to the table. Marge and Delores joined them. Not the slightest indication of their assignation passed between Marge and Bud.

Bob called, "Last call."

"Let's go to Rocky's and smoke a little," Jake said.

"Come on Bob, stay open. We don't want to go home!" Jake yelled back at him.

"Saturday we stay open till two. Come back then," Bob said. "Last call," he repeated.

Everyone drunkenly shuffled out. Cars headed in all directions, over grass, through one-way streets, and across double white lines.

Rubber burnt as tires fought for traction on wet roads. Bud was hunched over the steering wheel trying to see the road through blurred vision. Bev was in not much better condition than him.

When he reached The Box and was parking, their friends came by, inviting them to Rocky's. He and Bev obediently followed. Rocky's front door was wide open. They marched in. Rocky was in the center of the living room watching his girlfriend swinging from a cane chair suspended from the rafters. The hi-fi was blaring from a corner. Beer bottles, beer cans, and empty record covers were scattered all over. Bud and Bev fell onto the couch. He rested his feet on the cigarette-stained coffee table. Someone handed them each a beer. Bud felt as though he were suspended somewhere in space.

"Have a drag," Johnny said, holding a joint in front of Bud.

He took it, had a toke, and handed it to Bev. The joint passed between the three of them until it was a roach. Johnny ate the roach.

Shouts and laughter broke through the music. Rocky, naked, except for a large elephant leaf covering his genitals, was dancing, taking the leaf away periodically like the fan dancer Sally Rand at the Chicago World's Fair of 1933.

Everyone was making crude remarks. The girls feigned embarrassment. After the novelty wore off and no one was paying attention, Rocky disappeared into his bedroom with his girlfriend.

"Let's go to The Chateau," Tony called out.

The suggestion was unanimously approved, shouts of acquiescence preceded everyone's exit. Bud's legs were wobbly, his head throbbing. He followed blindly. Once again, cars perilously started in all directions before heading for The Chateau on A1A a few miles away. He pulled his MG into a parking space alongside Jake and Johnny. He and Bev squeezed into the elevator along with most of the beach bums. Sardines would not have been packed tighter. Fifteen floors up, they followed Max through the main dining room to a corner table overlooking the city. Lights flickered in the distance. Stars twinkled in the heavens. Bud had no idea where he was or how he got there, but he was enjoying himself.

"Buffet waiting. Let's go," someone said.

He grabbed Bev's hand as the line of beach bums headed for the buffet table. Someone thrust a plate in his hand. He started piling food on. He didn't know what he was putting on his plate, and as soon as it reached Mt. Everest proportions, Bev led him away. He couldn't taste the roast chicken, or the deviled eggs, or the coleslaw. He just shoveled it into his mouth, washing it all down with a cold beer, which had magically appeared.

The night wore on.

- 16 -

"Wake up. Wake up." The voice was shrill and distant.

Through bloodshot eyes Bev appeared in a hazy vision standing over him.

"It's 7:45 a.m. You have to be on the stand by eight," she said.

He knew she was speaking to him, but he couldn't hear anything but the throbbing in his head.

"Bud, get up. You have to get to the beach."

Then it clicked—*beach*—the key. His blurred vision and moribund senses cleared. Bev's face was returning to normal from the abstract Picasso he had been looking at. She led him to the shower. Slowly, the water revived him. Feeling was returning. Head was clearing. Vision was sharpening. He still felt terrible, but better than a few minutes ago. Bev handed him his lifeguard trunks after he stepped out of the shower. He needed help stepping into them. Using Bev's shoulder to balance himself, he got them on.

"I'll drive you to the stand," she said.

"No. I think I can do it," he said. His head was still pounding like a kettle drum. He tried not moving it.

Reluctantly, she agreed and lead him out of the apartment and down the stairs. The daylight blinded him the moment they stepped outside. Quickly, he reached into the glove compartment and put on his sunglasses. Relief. Things were still blurry, but the light didn't hurt as much. He kissed Bev gently, started his MG, and inched his way out of the parking space, heading for South 3, a little over two miles away. He was lucky no one else was on the road.

The beach was deserted. Not even the retirees were there. Collecting his gear, he set up the stand and settled down for his second day as a lifeguard. His only memory of last night was going to The Shack. Nothing else. The hours between then and now were blank.

Within minutes, he was fast asleep in his chair looking, for all intents and purposes, to be scanning the horizon. His sunglasses shielded his eyes. His safari hat, which was part of the gear he had inherited from the previous tenant of this stand, hid his face. The peace he so desperately needed was shattered by a high-pitched voice.

"Back again," the voice called. "Hey, I'm talking to you."

Lifting the safari hat from his face, he looked down to see the little blonde Lolita from yesterday standing there. He wasn't sure, but he was certain she was wearing a smaller bikini today. The shocking whiteness of it was all that Bud could see. What it wasn't hiding was anyone's guess. Essentials, if that.

"Yes, I'm back," he said.

"My name's Dee."

"Bud."

"You want some coffee?" she said. "You look like you could use it."

He nodded. She took off across A1A to a little greasy spoon diner. He wouldn't turn his head. It ached too much. *No more nights like last night*, he told himself. *I don't think I can take it.*

In the short time he had been on duty—he wasn't sure how long that had been, having left his watch in the apartment—the beach had attracted some people. Two families were settled not far from the water's edge. Children played in the surf. Sandcastles were being erected.

"Here," Dee said, holding a cardboard carrier with a steaming Styrofoam cup of coffee.

"Thanks," he said, taking it.

She stood watching, a supercilious grin covering her pretty face. The coffee slowly revived him, but her presence was disconcerting. He didn't know what to say and wanted solitude until he felt alive again. Her stoic presence was irritating.

"Are you going back to school?" she asked.

"Finished," he answered, laconically.

"Graduated, did you?"

"No. Three years."

"Yeah, well, then you'll love the beach."

"What's that supposed to mean?"

"Nothing. Nothing at all. I spend every day on it."

"What about you and school?" he asked, sarcastically, hoping that she would leave.

"Last year. Then I'm through."

"You're kidding." She didn't look old enough to be a senior.

"No. Both my parents are professors. I seem to have inherited some of their brains," she said, without guile.

"What about college?" he asked, immediately regretting that he'd prolonged the conversation he so badly wanted to end.

"I'm thinking about it. The sun's in my eyes. Why don't you jump down so I don't have to keep looking up?" She was persistent.

Reluctantly, he made a move, remembering what Dough said about tourists and a lifeguard's responsibility toward them. How old could she be, this five-foot attraction wrapped in the miniest bikini? Her piercing blue eyes shown like beacons against her dark tan and never wavered in their scrutiny of him. There was no insecurity in this Lolita but complete self-confidence, which added to his discomfort.

"Feeling better?" she asked.

"Coffee helped, thanks," he said. "Let me …" He reached for his carryall where his wallet was.

"No, it's okay," she cut in. "I'll take a cigarette off you when I need one. That'll make up for it."

"Okay."

She stood inches from him, her eyes glued to his. It was beginning to feel uncomfortable. His libido was rising. Time to check in. He grabbed the phone.

"Turner, South 3," he said.

Jake's voice bounced back to him. "Hey, old buddy, how you doing?"

"What the hell happened last night?" he asked. "I don't remember a thing."

"Nothing. No different than any other night."

"Where did we go?"

"The Shack."

"I know we went to The Shack. I mean after. I feel like the world blew up in my head."

"Too much drink."

"I've had more."

"Don't let it bug you. We do this all the time. You'll get used to it. Have to split. See you later." Jake hung up.

Bud looked at the phone link as if there were hidden answers in it.

"You must have had an unreal night," Dee said, smiling knowingly.

"Must have."

"What time do you break for lunch? Maybe I can have coffee with you?" she asked.

"Don't mention food," he said.

"You'd better take it easy," she said, advisedly.

"Thanks," he sarcastically answered.

"I'm serious. I don't mean to be blunt, but I've seen guys wreck themselves in a month down here. My brother did."

"Really?"

"Really. In his junior year at college, he took a job as a lifeguard. In no time, he was a beach bum. By the end of summer, he looked dead. My parents couldn't believe the physical change. He looked fifty. They sent him back to college two weeks early. This summer, he's been banished to Boston and postgraduate courses."

"He must have overdone it?"

"Obviously. He drank himself into oblivion. Not to mention some other goodies."

"What does that mean?"

"I think you know what I mean."

"For a little girl, you come on pretty strong."

"Do I? I thought I was being helpful."

"I think you know what I mean."

He headed up the beach, patrolling. She followed. He couldn't shake her. She was from Maryland. Her parents had moved to Ft. Lauderdale to get away from the bitter cold. They were fed up with the winter weather up North. She was seventeen and wanted to major in journalism. She'd already been published in the *Sun Sentinel*.

Her self-confidence impressed him. She must have inherited that from her parents. He was also impressed that she had been published. It was an article on teenagers being transplanted from one environment to another and how difficult it could be to make friends and adjust to another school. She was self-effacing about it, saying that it wasn't that the article was so good, but that the newspaper was doing a series on teenagers, and she happened to be lucky. He doubted it. From the way she comported herself, he was certain the article must have been lucid and highly competent.

"It's almost twelve thirty, and I'm getting hungry," she said. "If you don't want to eat, you can watch me."

He couldn't believe he'd been there four hours. It seemed like he just started.

"I'll have coffee," he said.

They went to Mary's. She ordered a hamburger and coke. He had coffee.

"How old is your brother?" Bud asked.

"Twenty-one."

"What's his major?"

"Not sure he has one. But he's smart. He'll make a choice shortly. It might be archaeology, like Dad."

He laughed out loud.

"What's that for?" she asked.

"Nothing. What you said reminded me of something."

They were finishing when Tony came in.

"Hi, buddy," Tony said coming up to the table.

"Hi," Bud said. "This is Dee."

"Hello," he said, almost leering.

"Hi," she answered, in total control.

"That was some party last night, eh?" Tony said.

"To tell you the truth, I don't remember a thing," Bud said.

Tony sat. "Man, you were right in the middle of all of it. Rocky went by your end of the couch a lot."

"Tony, I spoke to Jake. He said nothing happened."

Dee listened, making no comment. She sipped her coke, a knowing look in her eyes.

"You might have had a little too much drink, but the grass didn't go to waste," Tony said.

"I don't remember the joints. I really must have been out of it." He checked the clock over the counter. "I have to get back." Dee dropped some bills on the table.

"Right," Tony said.

Bud and Dee headed out. Tony's eyes never left Dee's amble proportions.

"You're too much, Bud. You really are," he said.

Bud waved him off. He led Dee outside.

"Playboy," Dee said, crossing A1A.

"What do you mean?"

"Rich. Nothing to do. Arrogant."

"I guess you're right."

"Guys like that bore the hell out of me."

"Same here. But he's not really a bad guy. Just have to get used to him."

"Who wants to?"

The beach had filled in the last hour.

"Thanks for the company," Dee said.

Bud took his position on the stand. "Anytime," he said.

"Is that a promise?"

Their eyes met. There was no hiding the hidden meaning behind her words. Her eyes held the proof.

"See you around," she said.

"Later," Bud said, returning his concentration to the beach.

- 17 -

It was worrying what Tony had said and what Jake did not say. He'd smoked a joint or maybe more, which he didn't remember. The first time he'd had a joint was before high school graduation, four years ago. He couldn't see what all the fuss was about. It didn't do anything to him, he thought. He got high, but not the big high everyone said you should get. He remembered those times getting high, but last night was a blank. Worse was Jake's casual assessment that nothing out of the ordinary had happened. It was worrying being so hedonistic about something so consequential. If drinking oneself into oblivion and getting high was considered normal, then maybe he should rethink his behavior.

    The afternoon dragged on. He answered tourists' questions with the aplomb of a diplomat, making points for Lauderdale, knowing he was more than likely incorrect in many of his responses. The saving grace was that most of the queries were innocuous. "Where is the cheapest restaurant? How do I get to I-95? How far is Miami from here? No one would suffer ill consequences. His station emptied. Most of the people knew the rules of the beach. If they swam out to the marking buoy, the furthest any swimmer was allowed to go, Bud would whistle them back, assuring their safety. The undercurrent was tricky that far out. No need to tempt fate. He had his station under control. Checking in with headquarters at five as required, Cummins checked him out. He packed up his gear and took off.

There was a note from Bev on the coffee table. She had gone shopping. He had a shower, then lay on the couch, falling into a light sleep. He heard Bev come in a short time later carrying groceries.

"Feeling better?" she asked, going into the kitchen.

"I need two days to recover."

"Tonight, we sleep. I just about made it through the day."

She made dinner: salad, lamb chops, and green beans, which they ate, with minimum conversation, at the small table overlooking the beach, both exhausted. Bev fell asleep immediately after. Bud lay awake thinking about Dee's dire warning about beach life, and Jake's nihilism, "We do this all the time. You'll get used to it."

- 18 -

With a good night's sleep, Bud started another day on Beach Patrol. His eyes didn't burn, his head was clear, he had energy. Bev helped him on his way with coffee and a kiss. It gave him the impetus to get started.

"Dough and I are going to the Dolphins game tomorrow," Bud said over coffee.

"I know," she responded.

"What's Miami like?"

"I've only been there once. For my ABC card."

"ABC card?" Bud said.

"Alcoholic Beverage Card. You need one to serve liquor."

"Oh." He finished his coffee, picked up his sunglasses and headed out.

"Don't fall asleep today," she said, jokingly.

"Not today. I feel like I could swim the English Channel. I'm full of energy."

Compared to the last two days, the beach was crowded for an early morning. But then again, it was Saturday. He had to pass his usual parking spot to find a place. Weekends must be hell. Twenty blankets already dotted the sandy landscape. A steady stream of people continued. By eleven thirty, there wasn't space for another blanket. Bud made periodic trips to the water, whistling in swimmers who were out too far. He left at twelve thirty for lunch at Mary's, hungry after yesterday's semi fast. He had a hamburger and coffee and treated himself to a piece of key lime pie. He felt good. Confident. His past indiscretions behind him. Nothing could interfere with his happiness. He headed back cheerfully humming to himself. When he reached the stand, the phone was ringing.

"Turner, South 3," he said.

It was Cummins. "I'm leaving early today. I thought I'd call and tell you you're on South 7 Monday."

The Sand Box. He smiled pleasantly knowing he'd be right across from Bev.

"Thanks," he said.

"Enjoy the game tomorrow," Cummins disconnected.

Bud jumped onto the stand pleased that he was fitting in so easily. In less than two weeks, he had made friends, found a job, and had a girlfriend. He liked the beach. It meant freedom to him. There were a few people to thank for that.

Dough had showed him kindness and friendship. He'd mentored him. He was like his guardian angel steering him in the right direction. He saw himself like Dough eventually, independent, confident, unrestrained by convention. He had chosen a career as lifeguard, risen to the top, and was a success. Everything Bud aspired to.

His one concern, Dough's strange behavior in his office. Bud was certain there was a logical explanation. Dough would explain it all in due course. Then he remembered Dough had acted puzzling one other time. When he'd asked about becoming a guard, and Dough suggested he'd be better off going home.

Bud wasn't going to conjecture what this meant. When Dough wanted to talk, he would listen. He'd been helping him all along. Bud was sure there was a reasonable explanation.

The other guards made him feel like he was part of a big family. He had been accepted immediately. It was as though he'd known them all his life. People he had grown up with. That there was a bond between them. They would be there for him under all circumstances. A fraternity. It was a feeling he'd not had before. He was certain he'd made the right decision to leave home, and fortunate to have found a home in Ft. Lauderdale.

Max: a bear of a man with a heart as big. He was the protector of all the beach bums. If there was anything Bud needed, he was sure Max would be there to help.

And Bev. He had become part of her life quickly. She gave him security and love. He wasn't sure what he felt was love, but he knew he wanted to be with her. He was glad he had come to Lauderdale. This was his future. He was sure of it. From now on, Lauderdale was his life.

His legs were cramping. He walked to the water's edge for exercise. Johnny was coming down the beach.

"You look happy," Johnny said.

"I feel great."

"For this time of year, there're sure as hell a lot of people on the beach. I don't think I've ever seen it like this," Johnny remarked.

"It's beautiful. Why should they stay away?"

"Because we have to keep an eye on them, that's why."

"That's our job," Bud told him.

"You'll see, "Johnny responded. "Wait till the season starts. You can't keep your eyes on everyone. All you need is one bad one and you'll wish you never were a guard. And those college kids are crazy when they hit this place."

"Let me tell you about the time I almost quit," Johnny continued. "I was on South 6, eyes peeled. It was during the high season. The beach was packed. This big college kid comes by, asks me if he could swim to the first coral reef. I said when I left at five he could swim to Europe. He said it was almost five, so what the hell was another half an hour? I told him that while I was on duty, he couldn't swim any further than I thought was safe and pointed out the marker buoy. He called me a fucking asshole, then said that if he wanted to swim to the coral reef, there was nothing I could do about it. The only way to stop him was to hit him, he said, but it better be a good shot because he was going to break my head if I didn't.

"Dough told us if we ever run into someone like this, just ignore them; let them get their rocks off, not start anything. It wasn't our job

The Slow Wave

to offend people on the beach no matter what they did. It was our job to watch them. Call for backup if you need it. So, I just sat there wishing this big shit would go away, but he keeps calling me names, daring me to get down off the stand. I ignored him, but I wanted to hit this bastard so hard it hurt. After about five minutes, he reaches up and grabs my foot. That's all I needed. I was on him so fast he didn't know what happened.

"I hit and kept hitting him until someone pulled me off. I had to see Cummins. He said I should take the next few days off to cool down. He was going to review the incident. Cummins said I should've called for backup before I let it go as far as it did. I was in a lot of trouble. My job was on the line. I was ready to quit right there, but Dough pulled me out of the office and told me to take the days off. He would speak to Cummins. I went to Miami, got bombed out of mind for three days, and then came back. The big fucking ox did swim to the coral reef while I was in Miami, drunk out of his mind. Must have hit his head on the reef. He washed up on the beach dead the next day. I went back to work as though nothing had happened. Dough and Cummins never spoke about it again."

"Why didn't you quit?"

Johnny hesitated." I had no place to go," he said, and headed back to his station without looking at Bud.

- 19 -

It was almost five. Bud collected his gear, depressed by what he had just heard.

He stopped at The Box to have a beer. Delores and Marge were there. Marge greeted him nonchalantly, as though nothing ever happened between them. Bev was upstairs. Tony came in, sat next to him.

"What do you say, old buddy?" he said, loudly slapping him on the back. "That was some piece of ass you were with yesterday."

Bud stared at him with contempt. How could this guy be for real? He was obnoxious. Tactless. Boring. He never had a good word to say about anyone. His motor mouth was going all the time. Bud finished his beer, ignoring him.

"Omar's is having a session tonight. Coming?" Tony continued, oblivious to Bud's indifference.

It was impossible to get away from this guy. He just kept nagging.

"I don't know. I'll ask Bev," Bud said.

"Oh, hell man, she'd dig it. She likes to dance."

"I'll ask her anyway," Bud told him.

"Okay. But if you don't come, you'll miss one of the most beautiful pieces of ass in the world," Tony boasted.

Bud's patience snapped. "Tony, why the hell do you always have to have the best of everything? Why is it that you never keep your mouth shut? And how the hell did you ever get to Lauderdale without being killed?" Sarcasm was dripping from every word.

Tony smiled, laughed lightly, and lit a cigarette.

"These Okies down here wouldn't know the truth from a hole in the ground. Does it matter if I exaggerate? Who's going to care? These silly bitches love to go out with money. And I got it. In spades."

"Right, but do you have to keep telling us about it? We believe you." Then an exasperated Bud told him, "I just don't get you. Sometimes you're okay; other times I wish you never existed."

"Bud, I like you. You're good people," Tony said as if Bud had been talking to a wall. Nothing Bud said seemed to have penetrated Tony's thick skull. "Let me buy you a drink."

"You're too much, Tony. You really are," Bud said, in frustration. He left Tony sitting there nursing his beer.

Bev was in the kitchen. She told Bud to get ready for a surprise. He jumped in the shower. Minutes later, looking at himself in the mirror, he was surprised to see how tan he was.

"It's ready!" Bev shouted. "Close your eyes. And don't peek."

"What is it?" Bud asked.

"Never mind. Just keep them closed until I say you can open them."

He stood in the middle of the room, a towel wrapped around him. Bev walked by and he heard her put something on the coffee table. She'd lit a match.

"Now," she said.

Bud opened his eyes. On the coffee table was a small cake with one candle.

"What's the occasion?" he asked.

"Your second full week in Lauderdale."

He took her in his arms, kissing her passionately.

"You little nut," he said.

"I knew you'd like it."

"Like it? I love it. I don't know what to say."

"Don't say anything," she said. "Eat."

– 20 –

Omar's was jam-packed. There were people everywhere. And this was the off season! The regulars were together: Marge, Delores, Jimmy, Ann, Judy, Windy. The beer was flowing. The music blasting. Bev was trying to say something to Bud, but the deafening music interfered. In desperation she shouted into his ear.

"Bob has invited everyone to The Shack tonight. He's bought some new restaurant furniture and it needs wear and tear," she said.

It was an inadequate excuse. If Bob had bought a place in Lauderdale, rather than Dania, the beach bums would frequent it more. The Shack was too far away to be convenient. Inducements like free beer were necessary. But the main reason the beach bums didn't want to go was the trepidation of driving through Dania. Bud would find out why to his dismay.

It was almost twelve. Jimmy suggested they get to The Shack before the beer got to them.

"Remember, Dania isn't the place you want to get stopped for DWI," he said.

"How right you are!" people shouted.

They made their way out through the crowd.

"See you at The Shack," Windy said and sped off down the deserted A1A with Delores and Marge, followed by the others.

***

Max was sitting at the bar, preoccupied, drinking by himself when Bud and Bev came in. Cass was drying glasses. A few tourists were at the bar. They asked him to come to The Shack. "I have a few things to do here. I'll see you later," he said. They left.

Rocky was outside, leaning against the building finishing a beer, barely able to stand.

"Hey Rocky, come to The Shack with us," Bud said.

"Later," he said, throwing the empty beer bottle across A1A onto the beach. He weaved from side to side, disappearing into The Box.

"Let's wait. He can't drive," Jimmy said.

"Okay," Bud responded.

Rocky started yelling. "I don't need no wop bastard telling me what to do!"

"Rocky, you're drunk. Why don't you go sleep it off?" Max calmly told him.

"No, I'm not. Don't tell me to leave."

Bud started in. Bev grabbed his arm.

"I like both those guys. I can't let them start killing themselves," Bud said.

Bud got between them.

"Come on Rocky, let's go to The Shack," he said.

"I don't want to go to the fucking Shack. I want to stay right here," Rocky growled.

"Why won't you go, Rocky?" Max asked.

"No one's going to tell me what to do," Rocky said, pushing Bud away.

"You'd better leave, Bud. He's drunk as hell," Max said.

Rocky yelled, "Give me a beer!"

People in the bar shouted for him to quiet down. Rocky told them to fuck off. A big, muscular sailor set his beer mug down with a bang.

"Shut your fucking mouth!" the sailor shouted.

Rocky was on him in an instant. The sailor tumbled to the floor. Rocky's fists were pounding away but missing their mark. Obscenities filled the air. The sailor easily pushed Rocky off him and got to his feet.

"You fucking bastard," the sailor said, punching Rocky, who tried getting up but was knocked back down with another punch.

Bud made a move to help. Max restrained him. "One on one," Max said, holding Bud.

Rocky was on the floor, trying to rise, shouting all the time. "You cocksucking sea fish." Getting to his feet, he grabbed a bar stool, lifting it as a weapon. The sailor pushed it away easily and hit Rocky with a powerful punch. He went down heavily. Blood immediately appeared on his face. He was holding his eye, blood coming through his fingers. The sailor calmly picked up his change, cigarettes, and lighter, and left.

"Next time shut your fucking mouth," he said, and was gone.

Bud and Max knelt to help Rocky. Blood was all over the floor and on his clothes. The tourists had left. Bev held her hands to her face in anguish. The sight of so much blood was sickening.

"Rocky, Rocky," Max said.

Rocky was semi-conscious, breathing heavily, blood coming from his forehead. Cass threw Max a towel. He wiped Rocky's face. There was a big gash across the top of the left eye.

"He must have hit the bar on the way down," Max said.

Bev turned away, not able to look. She felt like vomiting. Bud led her outside, sat her on the bumper of his MG, cradled her in his arms.

Jimmy came out. "Max is taking Rocky to the hospital," he said.

Jimmy squeezed into the back of Bud's MG. Bud silently drove to The Shack.

***

Bud waited for Dough to pick him up outside The Box. The blood had been cleaned away. There were no signs that a fight had taken place last night.

Dough pulled up. "Get in," he called.

Bud was silent, playing over the events of last night. Dough sensed Bud's preoccupation but did not intrude. He drove at a steady speed to Miami.

Bud had seen fights in college, but not as bloody as last night. Or as serious. It shocked him. Rocky almost lost his eye. He let Bev sleep so he would not have to discuss it. Even on the drive back from The Shack last night nothing was said. They both had fallen asleep with their own fears and apprehensions.

As the game progressed, Bud's disposition lightened. By the end of the game and the Dolphins' victory, Bud was almost back to normal. Dough knew to leave Bud alone until he came around on his own. Bud told Dough about the fight, which he already knew about. Max called after taking Rocky to the hospital. There was no way he would be fit to work. Dough would have to find a temporary replacement. Dough let Bud talk the whole incident through. He surmised the reasons for Rocky's erratic behavior. They weren't that much different than his.

Dough had been with the Beach Patrol since he was seventeen years old. He was thirty-seven, divorced, the father of a son, who lived with his mother in LA. He'd met his ex-wife on the beach in Santa Monica after getting out of the Army where he was a lifeguard at the base pool at Ft. Ord in Northern California. They moved to Lauderdale when some of his lifeguard friends suggested they change scenery. He stayed in Lauderdale after the divorce.

His wife had wanted to leave Lauderdale and go back to California. She never really liked Lauderdale. Dough was in line for supervisor and felt they should stay. Six months later the promotion still had not materialized. They grew further apart and reluctantly he agreed to give LA another try. He returned to Beach Patrol in Santa Monica. The opportunity for advancement wasn't as good as in Lauderdale. He wanted to return. She didn't want her son to become a beach bum like his father, she told him. Opportunities were far greater in Los Angeles than in Ft. Lauderdale, and she wanted their son to have those opportunities.

She never really liked him being a lifeguard; she thought he should go back to school and get a degree. He'd quit high school in his sophomore year to join the Army. In Lauderdale, he could make a better living, so he left. He made supervisor and hadn't seen his ex-wife and son since. What else could he do? Where else could he go? This was his life. The only thing he knew. He had no place to go, and more than likely, Rocky suffered the same fate. He was one of the lifeguards who went to Lauderdale with Dough years ago. It was a sobering thought to know you had wasted your life.

- 21 -

Guarding South 7 was exciting and fun. Everyone he knew passed by during his shift. Bons mots were tossed back and forth like confetti. Nights of extreme liquor and drug indulgence were characterized with banal quips. The Rocky incident was forgotten by the end of the week. No one mentioned it. It was as though it had never happened. Nothing inimical ever stayed with the beach crowd. Life was too short to dwell on hardship. None of the beach crowd wanted reminders of the ennui their life had taken. The only evidence was eighteen stitches Rocky carried on his forehead. He asked Cummins for medical leave, saying he hit his head on his steering wheel breaking fast to avoid an accident.

Bud could barely get out of bed after spending most nights drinking at Omar's, The Shack, and The Box. His social life was a never-ending whirlwind, ending with a late-night breakfast at The Chateau. By the end of the month, he had lost fifteen pounds and could hardly stay awake during the day. After work, he showered, took a two-hour sleep, and was ready to face the night again. He had become a beach bum.

***

The letter was addressed to him, sent care of The Box. It was from his mother in answer to the single post card he had written telling her where he was, what he was doing, and that he was all right. It was succinct. She thanked him for his card and asked him to write more.

She said nothing had changed since he'd been gone, and that Sheila asked for him all the time. A PS at the bottom said his college exam marks had arrived. They were good. He tucked it in his carryall, not giving it a second thought.

Bev was picking up Bud's denims when the letter fell out. She picked it up, noticed it was from Ames, and put it on the coffee table.

"Mother, asking me to write more often," Bud said.

Bev smiled strained acknowledgement. Bud sensed the sadness immediately. He cradled her in his arms, not understanding what had happened. Tears fell on his arm.

"What's the matter?" he asked.

"Nothing," she said, trying to move away. He held her.

"Why the tears? What brought this on? Not the letter? Was it the letter?" he asked.

She didn't answer and sat on the couch, holding her face in her hands as she cried.

"I'll read it to you. It's only a few lines from my mother," he said.

"I believe you," she said.

"Then why all the tears?"

"It's stupid. It'll pass."

"What's stupid?" He would not accept such a lame excuse.

"When I saw the letter, it reminded me of home. I haven't spoken to my mother in a year. I know I'm being stupid, childish, but it was a shock seeing that letter. I haven't thought of home in months," she said.

"It's not stupid," he said, cradling her in his arms. "Look, I have a great idea. Let's drive up the coast and have dinner. We need a change."

Bev kissed him and wiped away tears. "Okay, you wonderful nut," she said.

They drove up A1A in silence. Bud concentrating on the road. Bev lost in thought. The last time she spoke to her family was over a year ago. She'd told her mother she left her job in Chicago and was in Lauderdale. Her mother was surprised and pleaded with her to come home. She said she needed space and when she was settled and had her life in order, she would decide. Her mother wanted to know what happened. Bev lied, saying she needed a change. The job had put her under a lot of pressure, which she needed a break from. She was okay. She would be in touch.

She wrote one letter, saying she was staying in Lauderdale, then nothing. Her mother wrote every month for the first six months, but after not hearing from her, stopped, hoping Bev's senses would return. After all she had a degree in art and design. Her whole future was before her. The important job at BBD&O in Chicago had proved that. Bev was on her way to success. She couldn't understand what had gone wrong, and she was worried. Their last conversation ended in an argument, which neither won.

Bev knew she should have written explaining her failed relationship, but her strict Catholic upbringing caused her embarrassment. Her family, especially her mother, would not condone having an affair with a married man, much less living with him. She was not raised that way. Sex before marriage was forbidden by the seventh commandment. She knew her mother would be heartbroken if she found out. She thought time would heal the embarrassment, but it didn't. Every time she thought of Chicago, the image of her un-catholic behavior showed itself. What helped was becoming part of the decadent beach crowd. They were her family now. Their hedonistic lifestyle helped her forget. Within two months of being in Lauderdale, Chicago was forgotten, and she felt alive and free again. She hadn't thought of Tom Callahan in months. She'd heard from friends in Chicago that he had started another relationship at the agency very shortly after she left. It was the final admission that he had been lying to her about getting married. Then Bud showed up and everything was perfect.

"Hey, where are you?" Bud asked.

Bev's reverie broke. "I was just thinking. I'm still here," she said.

"You were miles away. I could feel it."

"Well, I'm back now," Bev said, but something had changed.

They drove to Palm Beach, had dinner overlooking the sea, and talked about the beach, about how they both liked their jobs and about how they fit so well together. They didn't talk about their past or their future. The conversation was superficial but safe. Both had things they wanted to hide.

He was accepted by the beach crowd. Being a lifeguard required little and offered a lot. There was a future to it. It was also like being your own boss. Bud couldn't ask for more. College was a thing of the past. He had found a home.

- 22 -

Windy was coming down the street as they drove up to The Sand Box.

"What's up?" he asked.

"Just had dinner," Bud said.

"I'll buy you a beer," Windy said.

"You go. I have a few things to do," Bev told him.

"I'll be right up." Bud said.

Bev disappeared down the street.

"She's great people," Windy said.

"How right you are," Bud responded.

The Box was nearly empty. A few tourists sat at the bar. Bud and Windy sat near the door.

"How long you been here now?" Windy asked.

"I'm not sure. Six weeks, maybe a little longer."

"I've been here six years. What do you think of that?"

It seemed a rhetorical question. Bud sipped his beer, waiting for Windy to continue.

"Six years. You know when I first came here, I thought this was the only way to live. All the girls you wanted. Freedom. No responsibilities. No one telling you what to do. What a life. What a waste," Windy said.

Bud was surprised by the self-pity. To him living in Lauderdale was like paradise. He couldn't understand Windy criticizing it.

"I'm sorry. I'm thinking out loud," Windy said, when he saw the puzzled look on Bud's face.

"It's okay. Sometimes it pays to hear yourself think," Bud said, trying to lighten the atmosphere.

"Yeah. You're right. Have another beer."

"No thanks. Bev's waiting."

"Right. Take it easy. See you tomorrow."

On the way back the apartment, Bud thought over what Windy said. Had he wasted six years of his life? What he'd said about Lauderdale was true: women, freedom, no responsibility. Why was that a waste of life? Whatever it was, it didn't apply to him. He was not Windy. What mistakes Windy had made, Bud wouldn't. These were the best years of his life. A time to have fun. To be frivolous. He had his whole life ahead of him.

***

Bev had changed clothes, ready to face the night, fresh and energetic. They hit Omar's, The Shack, and The Sand Box. They also spent some time at Rocky's, and by one thirty, they were at The Chateau. At the first sign of the rising sun, exhausted and slightly drunk, they went home to enjoy the pleasure of their own company.

- 23 -

Bud had been on the stand an hour. The beach was still deserted except for one or two couples. The Box was closed. No cars on A1A. The sky was clear, a promise of a perfect day. Bud leaned back in his chair, exhausted.

He lost his balance but righted himself before falling. Sometime later, he wasn't sure how long, he woke from a deep sleep. The sky had darkened. The wind was at gale force. The surf was pounding the shore. Groggy still from last night, he pulled himself together and called headquarters asking for the weather report. Cummins told him rain, getting heavier as the day wore on. Possible hurricane warning. He could pack up until it was over. Bud stowed his gear in the MG. Thunder clapped overhead. The heavens opened. Rain pelted down in sheets so dense he couldn't see across A1A.

He headed for The Box when Dee, the little Lolita from South 3, pulled up in a red Mustang. She waved him over. He got in drenching wet.

"There was sun. You should have been here earlier," Bud said.

"Funny," she said. "What are you going to do? You're soaking wet."

"Wait till it stops. Then get back on the job."

"Let's have some coffee while you wait," she said, pulling into light traffic. "There's a towel in the back."

"Thanks," he said reaching for it.

"Where to?" she asked.

"Anywhere. But not too far. Just as soon as this stops, I have to be back on station."

He did the best he could drying himself and patting down his rain-soaked T-shirt and bathing trunks.

She continued on A1A, driving cautiously, the rain sleeting against the windshield. The wipers could do little.

"How's the lifeguard from Ames?"

"Okay. What are you doing out in weather like this?"

"As you said, sunny before."

She was wearing hip huggers, exposing part of her belly, which was flat and hard. A light see-through pullover covered her bikini top. Her breasts stood proud and firm underneath. There was three to four inches between the hem of the pullover and the hip-huggers. Every time she hit the brakes they bounced. Bud had to turn away before his staring became too obvious.

Nothing was open. Even Mary's was closed.

"I have an idea," Dee said and drove toward the residential section of Ft. Lauderdale.

She pulled into the driveway of a nondescript stucco house with blue window shutters, parked next to a black VW Beetle.

"That's mother's. She must still be here," Dee said, opening the screen door. "Mom. Mom," she called.

Bud followed her through the kitchen, into the living room.

"I'm in the bedroom," called a voice from the other end of the house.

"I brought a friend," Dee called out. "Make yourself comfortable. I'll make coffee." She disappeared into the kitchen.

The living room was furnished in replica early American, heavy wood furniture with oversized cushions. It reminded him of the living room from the TV show *Bonanza*. Bookshelves lined the walls. Children's pictures hung on one wall. A TV console sat against another wall. A patio ran the length of the room overlooking a garden, which ran down to the canal where a small outboard motorboat was moored. Bamboo furniture was dotted around outside on the well-manicured lawn.

"It'll be ready in minute," Dee said returning to the living room.

She'd changed into a light cotton T-shirt, with "Ft. Lauderdale" printed across the front with "a bikini-clad sun worshiper" reclining under the letters. Her hair was tied in a ponytail. She looked even younger. Her ample proportions bursting to be free, Bud pulled his eyes away from the mimesis, Lolita.

"Daddy built the patio. He's very good with his hands. He can fix anything."

"Nice," Bud said. His father had also built a patio onto their living room, and they had a large garden too. Nostalgia spread through him at the thought.

"Hello, I'm Mrs. Fowler," Dee's mother said, introducing herself. She was an attractive woman in her early forties, with the same coloring and proportions as her daughter. But she was four to five inches taller, thus able to wear her endowments much more discreetly.

"Bud Turner."

"Yes, I know. Dee's mentioned you," she said. "Sorry, I can't stay. Neither rain nor sleet, as the postman's motto goes. Faculty meetings take precedent over any kind of weather." She left, pecking Dee on the cheek.

"Pretty, isn't she?" Dee said.

"Yes," Bud said as he sat on the couch.

"She's as hip as a teenager. Keeps up with everything going on. Wait till you meet dad. He's a big kid. They're a wild pair."

Bud nodded. It was obvious this family was caring and loving. A far cry from his. The thought was disquieting.

"I'll get the coffee," Dee said. "Milk? Cream?"

"Black."

He concentrated on the outside, letting his thoughts wander.

Dee came back carrying two steaming mugs of coffee.

She sipped hers, keeping her eyes on Bud. "You must have been miles away," she said.

"When?"

"A few seconds ago. I was asking if you wanted sugar. You were staring out the window. I was calling you, and nothing. Totally preoccupied."

"Didn't hear you."

"I know. Miles away."

"I guess."

The rain was still pelting down. The more time he spent with this Lolita, the more surprised he was by her self-confidence, demeanor, and perception.

"Where are you?" she asked.

"I'm sorry. I seem to be drifting off." He took a sip of coffee. "What did you tell your mother about me?"

"That I met a lifeguard named Bud, and that he reminded me of someone."

"Anyone I know?"

"Not yet. But you'll meet him as soon as he's home from school."

"Your brother?"

"No."

"Who then. The suspense is killing me."

"My father," she said.

"Do I look that old already?" he asked.

"Of course not. You'll see. He's very much like you."

"And what am I like?"

"It's hard to explain. It's more of a feeling."

Bud laughed to himself. If she knew what he was thinking, he doubted if he would remind her of her father.

"What's that look mean?"

"Nothing. Nothing. Just smiling."

She talked about her parents, where they came from, what subjects they taught—father archaeology, mother American history—and how long they've been in Lauderdale. He wasn't listening. The situation was ironic to him. He was sitting with a seventeen-year-old whom he wanted to fuck, and he was sure she knew it. But instead of being coy, like most seventeen-year-olds should be, she was confident, assertive, and attentive. That didn't bother him. What did was that, the longer she spoke and the longer they spent together, the less he wanted to fuck her. She oozed sexuality, but talking about her loving, productive family had the opposite effect of sexual intimacy. It brought to mind all the disaffection he had with his family. He set his cup down.

"I'll refill it," she said.

"No, that's all right. I've had enough."

Bud was uncomfortable. He wanted to kiss her, but something held him back. He stood at the window, looking at rain, nervous, undecided. The atmosphere was charged with unknown emotion. He turned. There was wanting there, he thought. He bent to kiss her. She moved her lips away.

"Why?" Bud asked.

"Why do you want to kiss me?'"

A surprise jolt went through him. Rejection? He had no answer to the simple question. He found her attractive. And he wanted to fuck her. But he didn't think that was the answer she was looking for. He had no answer.

"You win. I haven't got an answer," he said.

"I wasn't trying to win. I just want to know why you want to kiss me. There must be a reason."

"I just want to kiss you."

"It would be nice to kiss you. And I really want to. But I don't feel you want to. Not really."

Bud felt uncomfortable. This seventeen-year-old was rebuking him. He'd never thought this would happen in Lauderdale. The few times he'd been unfaithful to Bev were casual fucks. It didn't mean anything. Not to him. Not them. They wanted to fuck, and Bud accommodated them. Nothing was ever mentioned. They knew he was living with Bev. It didn't matter to them. They didn't want anything more. Neither did Bud. A quick fuck during lunch hour, or in the john at one of the hangouts.

He didn't feel guilty at being unfaithful. It was ubiquitous. All the guards did it, and so did the girls. But now this kid was making him confront his scruples. He could easily lie. Come up with some explanation. What difference would it make? But he couldn't. And he didn't know why. He had two choices: lie or leave, before he became more humiliated.

"Thanks for the coffee," he said. "I have to get back."

She took a beat or two before answering, as if knowing his thoughts. "I'm sorry you can't meet Dad. You'd like him," she said.

"I'm sure I would. Some other time."

They drove in silence to his station. There wasn't any tension in the car. More of relief. Dee could see how deflated his ego was and did not want a confrontation over what she had asked, and he had declined to give. She knew perfectly well that he wanted to fuck her, but she needed more than a casual roll in the hay during a rain-soaked afternoon. If he had just been honest and said what was on his mind, other than showing weakness, she would have acquiesced, and they could have spent the afternoon in bed.

Bud got out of the car and Dee disappeared down A1A. The rain had slowed to a drizzle. Instead of calling in, he headed for the Act One bar down the street.

He gulped a scotch back and ordered another. He felt like shit. His mind was reeling. What had just happened? Why was he feeling like this? It wasn't that important. Just some kid. Nothing. But it was bothering him. He belted back two more Scotches. The effect was slowly incapacitating him. His senses were dulling, his thinking foggy. He hadn't eaten. The alcohol was coursing through his system fast. He began seeing images—images of Bev, the beach, back home, Sheila, Omar's, the Box, The Shack. They were all jumbled together like a finger painting. Dough came into focus then vanished. The beach crowd appeared and disappeared. He saw himself falling, hitting the floor with a thud. Blood spurted up and over him like a blanket.

He felt arms lifting him, carrying him. Ocean air assailed his nostrils. Blurred lights glistened overhead. He was swaying back and forth. He bounced off something solid and slid to the ground, glad to be off his feet. He lay motionless enjoying the rest he so badly needed.

"Put him in the back. Watch his head."

He was carried and placed on something soft.

"Looks like a guard."

"Take him in. We'll check him out while he sobers up."

There were undistinguishable sounds. His body jerked back and forth. He was placed on something cold. He felt suspended. Floating. Then there was silence. He drifted off into a deep unnatural sleep.

He lay motionless on a dirty, rough, odious mattress. The stench of aged urine was overpowering. Insects awoke, sensed nourishment, and tasted the fresh morsel of food. They crept across his legs, down his pants, over his arms, into his hair. Here was food. They ate until sated. Sand fleas weaved in his hair nestling, secure in the warmth of body heat. Mosquitoes sucked, satisfying their appetites. Cockroaches crawled over him, their tentacles tasting the moisture of his body. Water bugs that lay dormant on the ceiling inched their way down the wall to explore this new object. He could feel nothing. He lay sleeping, breathing in sand fleas and mites. Bugs and vermin from every corner had found a new resting place, satisfying all their desires.

He stirred slowly scattering the tenants lodged on his body for the last ten hours. Cautiously uncurling himself from a web of unconsciousness, he wiped insects from his face. His head was a drum that wouldn't stop beating and grew louder with each movement. Through unfocused eyes, he saw bugs scurrying for safety. He made no move to expedite them, his senses not responding properly.

Standing, unsteady, on damp cement, he brushed himself off. Every motion another painful stab to his nervous system. Bugs were crawling away in all directions. He did not move, fearful of stepping on them with his bare feet.

He saw bars on the windows, the heavy steel door, the filthy mattress he had been sleeping on. In the corner was a rust-stained sink. He splashed water on his face letting it run down his body, bringing more life back to him. He was in jail. But where? He peered through the bars of the steel door. Nothing.

"Hello," he called.

Silence.

Then he said louder, "Hello."

"Okay, okay. I hear ya," a deep voiced Southern accent answered.

A tall, overweight, crew cut, uniformed guard came into view. The uniform was perfectly pressed, his badge shining brightly.

"Ya up, are ya?" the guard said with an accent so thick it was almost unintelligible.

"Where am I?" Bud asked.

"Fort Lauderdale. Where'd ya think?"

"When can I get out?"

"Court starts at eight."

"What time is it now?"

"Seven thirty."

Bud backed away against the wall, his body aching all over. Standing was difficult. He was thankful for the wall.

"Breakfast will be around any minute."

"Coffee, black," Bud said.

The guard left. Bud spied the toilet. He stood over it, hands outstretched against the wall, balancing himself. The pungent odor of urine filled his nostrils. The poison he put there yesterday streamed out. It took minutes as it burned its way through him. Steam rose from the bowl. He sat on the edge of the bed, shaking his head trying to clear it from the drumming, which continued in a slow, steady beat as he watched the biggest cockroach he had ever seen marching up the wall. He moved, squashing a water bug in the process. He turned the mattress over, awakening sleepy serpents underneath. They scurried away. He let the mattress fall crushing more of his guests. He stood, leaned against the wall waiting for the last of the vermin to scatter, then sat on the bunk resting his aching body against the wall with his feet propped up on the rim of the bunk for support.

Two sand fleas were scurrying across the mattress. They crawled over him disappearing under the bunk. He felt like vomiting. On the faded green walls was scribbled graffiti: "Jay Was Here. Piss on Ft. Lauderdale. Brownie Sucks, a great blow job," and an indecipherable phone number. Other graffiti had been scribbled out. The usual genitalia art work, both male and female, was also there. Surprisingly, it was excellent. High above, a dim forty-watt bulb was secure in a wire cage.

How easy it would be to tie something to that and swing freely, ending this nightmare, Bud thought to himself.

"Here's ya coffee," said the guard, setting the Styrofoam cup on the ledge of the cell door.

Bud carried it back to the bunk. The coffee had an acrid taste. It made him feel sicker. He put it on the floor, searched his pockets for a cigarette but only found a book of wet matches welded together. A large water bug was trying to crawl up the side of the coffee cup. It fell over splashing its contents over the floor. A never-ending stream of insects appeared from nowhere, bathing in the wetness.

Bud couldn't remember leaving Act One. All he could remember were the shot glasses coming one after the other, then he found himself here in this Kafkaesque prison. He would burn all the clothes he was wearing, shower for hours to wash away the stench and maybe the memory.

The guard opened the cell door. "Come on, court's starting."

Bud stepped into the corridor. The walls were a faded green, with years of use written on them. Blotches of water stain, like a mosaic, assailed him. A rust-stained sink hung on a wall. A mop leaning against it. Early morning sun streamed thought the barred window. It was depressing. The other tenants from the illustrious hotel, which would not be mentioned in any holiday brochure, appeared. A Black man of indeterminable age, hunched over like a pretzel, took his place in line behind Bud. Two White men years over forty, beards nicotine-stained and dripping saliva, their hair a nest for sand fleas and other insects and their stench overpowering, fell in behind the Black man. Their clothes, including sweat-stained shirts full of holes, were in such disrepair you couldn't tell the original color. The last out was an overweight White man somewhere in his middle thirties in a T-shirt and tan pants smoking a cigarette.

"Put out all butts. Sit in the chairs facing the judge as soon as you get into court. And no talking," the guard said.

He opened the huge, heavy oak doors leading to the courtroom. The first people Bud saw were Dough and Bev sitting in the first row of seats. A strained smile appeared on Bud's face as he took a seat next to the old men. It was worse than lying face down on the insect-infested bunk. He moved a few seats away.

The judge was already on the bench reading through some papers, his face so close his nose was touching them. He looked up over his half-moon glasses, glancing at his captives.

Bud was called first. He stood before the judge. A permanent sneer was etched on the judge's face. His glasses looked as if they were part of his ruddy face. He had no neck. His head sat on his shoulders like a growth. His black robe covered an enormous bulk. He reminded Bud of a huge dung heap with eyes. He started reading Bud's offenses in a slow monotone with a voice honed on years of cigarettes and whisky.

"Being drunk and disorderly in a public place. Resisting arrest. No identification at time of arrest. How do you plead?" The judge stared at Bud unflinching.

That many offenses? he thought. The only time he'd been in front of a judge was to pay a five-dollar parking ticket back home. He knew he'd done that. But this was unbelievable. He heard himself say, "Guilty."

The judge mumbled something, picking up some more papers. "For being drunk and disorderly, fifty dollars."

Bud went instantly cold.

"For resisting arrest, fifty dollars. For having no identification, fifty dollars. For booking and court costs, fifty dollars."

Bud couldn't move. He felt faint. His mouth was dry.

"Pay the bailiff," the judge ordered.

A policeman led Bud over to the bailiff. Dough and Bev were there. Dough paid the fine and they left. Bud was in shock.

He sat in the back seat of Dough's car. No one said anything. Bud couldn't even utter a thank you when they reached The Sand Box. Bud ripped his clothes off, threw them in pile outside the door and got in the shower, letting the hot water burn away the dirt and stench.

Welts left from insects covered his entire body. His hair still housed some. He scrubbed and washed viciously. Over and over, he shampooed his hair as if trying to wash away the memory. He came out of the bathroom feeling almost alive, but still in shock.

"Two hundred bucks," he said, as if in a trance.

Bev placed a cup of coffee on the table, compassion evident in her countenance.

"I don't believe it," he said. "I don't believe it."

Bev was silent. Not sure what his reaction would be.

"Bud …" she said.

"Not now. Not now."

Bud noticed the time. "Holy shit, nine thirty. I have to go."

He took his other pair of swim trunks from the drawer, bounding out the door. "Later," he said.

His gear was still in the MG. He hooked up the phone link and checked in with headquarters.

"Come see me during lunch," Cummins said.

"Yes, sir."

He jumped on the stand knowing he was in for a reprimand if not worse. There were a few people on the beach. The surf was calm. He'd have a lot of time to think. Dough came by a few minutes later.

"Let's take a walk," he said.

They walked up the beach along the water's edge.

"What happened?" Dough asked.

"I'm not sure. I was having a drink at Act One. Next thing I know, I wake up in jail."

"I received a call from the police telling me they thought they had one of our guards on a drunk charge. They said, the guy had no ID, so they didn't know who he was, but he was wearing a Ft. Lauderdale Beach Patrol swimsuit. They asked me to come down and verify it. You were out cold."

"I don't remember any of that."

"You were supposed to be on your stand, not in Act One."

"It was pelting down. Cummins told me to close the stand. I had a cup of coffee with someone, then stopped off for a drink to warm up. I don't know how I got bombed."

"The rain stopped at three, three thirty. When Cummins didn't hear from you, he called around. No one knew where you were."

"Dough, I can't remember the rain stopping. I can't even remember leaving Act One."

"I'm sure Cummins will want to see you. Tell him the truth. Try and remember what made you go into Act One. Something more substantial than what you told me."

"Cummins already called. I have to see him during lunch."

Dough jumped into the patrol jeep. "Don't worry about the money. You can pay me a few dollars every week."

"Thanks."

Some of the beach bums came by asking how he was and what he thought of Southern hospitality. He said he had a drum in his head and the hospitality was expensive. They made jokes about it, telling him they also had spent time in the pokey. He told them he was okay and that he was only worried about his meeting with Cummins. They told him not to. It wasn't that important. Bud wasn't that sure, but their insistence gave him confidence. He stopped off at The Box to see to Bev. The forlorn look on his face almost made her cry. She wished him luck and told him not to worry. She had already spoken to Max. There was a job for him if he needed it, and there was a strong possibility he would lose his current job.

"Bud, I have to make a report concerning your absence from your post yesterday. Anything you have to say in your defense would help," Cummins said.

"I left the stand just before lunch to have coffee with a friend, right after I spoke to you. It was still raining when I started back. I stopped for a drink. After that I don't remember a thing," Bud said.

"That's very ambiguous, Bud. Can't you be more specific?"

Bud didn't think his visit with Dee was that important. He'd only had a cup of coffee and then left. What could that have to do with what happened at Act One?

"Where did you go before Act One?"

He told Cummins he'd spent about an hour or so with Dee and her mother. As he talked, his memory came back. He knew what had caused his drinking, but he didn't tell Cummins. He only mentioned Dee and her mother, and leaving. He knew that saying anything about being with a seventeen-year-old alone in her house wasn't what Cummins wanted to hear. It would be obvious what he was up to. Mentioning it wouldn't help his case.

"I'm going to put you on probation for a while, Bud. But if anything like this happens again, I'll have to let you go."

"Thank you, sir. I give you my word it will not happen again. And I'm sorry it happened in the first place."

"Okay. Report back to your station."

Bud walked out feeling as though a big weight had been lifted from his back. He still had his job.

Cummins had heard all types of excuses and stories in his years as Commissioner of Parks and Recreation. He prided himself on good judgment. It was obvious to him that Bud was depressed meeting a family of obvious contentment. In all likelihood, it reminded him of his family and the problems he was escaping. Many of the young lifeguards who passed through Lauderdale suffered the same. Bud's way of coping with it was to have a drink. Cummins was certain that the consequences of having that drink would be enough to keep Bud out of his office. He put Bud's file away and called Dough to tell him his decision.

- 24 -

Bud had little money to spare, but he would give Dough a few dollars on account. He was still shocked that the fine was so big. Bev explained that was how the county makes its money. Heavy fines for anything to do with the police, such as public drunkenness, vagrancy, sleeping on the beach, you name it, and they had a fine for it. In her opinion he got off light, more than likely because he was a lifeguard. The heaviest fines were for traffic violations. She had heard about fines for hundreds of dollars for speeding, going through red lights, or just parking in a no parking zone. That was why none of the lifeguards liked going to The Shack. Getting caught speeding through Dania could cost you a month's paycheck. The one consolation that came out of this whole mess was that Bud still had his job.

The rest of the day was spent at his station talking to the other guards who came by. They made jokes about his night in jail, and soon, even Bud was. That evening, Jake, Rocky, and Johnny came over to the apartment. Beer and joints went around. Bev fixed something to eat, then they took off for Omar's and The Shack. By the end of the evening, Bud had forgotten about Dee, jail, and his depression. He was bought beers up and down the beach. Arriving home after an early morning breakfast at The Chateau, Bud didn't even look at the pile of dirty clothes outside the door. Beach life had returned to normal.

- 25 -

As the weeks passed, Bud's misadventure was forgotten. No one mentioned it. He put it out of his mind as if it never happened. His patrol stations changed every week working up and down the beach. He was involved in all the social events going on and got to know everyone even remotely connected to the beach crowd. He was a regular at all the bars and cheap restaurants, Mary's being everyone's first choice. It was as though he had been in Lauderdale all his life. Paying Dough every week was a financial strain, but he managed. His and Bev's relationship was secure. She never questioned his staying out with the guards all night. She knew the ways of the beach bums. She didn't like it but reluctantly accepted it. Making love to Bev was different. He didn't enjoy sleeping with the others as much as he did with Bev, but he wasn't going to forego a fuck because of some unwritten rule about fidelity. He had unconsciously adopted the hedonistic ways of the beach bums. And they washed over him like a slow wave gathering force before it crashed and disappeared as though it never existed.

- 26 -

He hadn't seen Dee since that fateful day. The memory faded. He was living moment to moment, too busy to clutter up his mind with trivialities. Although every night was the same, it was different. There was always the unexpected. That was the excitement of living on the beach. There was always something going on.

- 27 -

He was on South 3 when Laura came walking by. She wasn't pregnant, but he hadn't heard she'd given birth. He found out that she'd had a miscarriage. She hadn't even gone to the hospital. No one knew where she was living. Later that day, at the edge of the private property marker, he noticed her sleeping, rolled up like a ball. He stowed his gear in his car without giving her another thought.

Bud was at The Box when Tony came in, boisterous as ever. He sat down and ordered a beer. He'd spent the last few days in Miami shacking up with a stewardess, hitting all the night spots. He was going to bring her back to Lauderdale, but she had to fly back to Boston. Bud nodded, bored. Tony's exploits were a joke on the beach. No one believed him and could not care less.

Rocky came in. The stitches had been taken out. He was back on duty. A thin scar was all that was evident above his eye. He sat at the bar, ordered a beer.

"Windy left," he said.

"What do you mean, he left?" Bud asked.

"Town. Lauderdale. He left two days ago. Didn't Dough tell you?"

"No. Where did he go? "Bud said.

"Didn't say. Just picked up his check Friday and split," Rocky said, sipping his beer.

Bud didn't remember Windy saying anything about leaving. He finished his beer and told Bev he'd see her later.

Dough lived a few blocks from The Box in a one-bedroom apartment. It was sparsely furnished with a wicker chair, wicker couch, throw cushions, and a Formica table with two chairs. A king-size bed was in the bedroom along with a single chest of drawers. Dough invited him in, offered him a beer, and returned to watching a replay of a Dallas football game on the TV.

"When did Windy get walking fever? "Bud asked, taking a seat on the couch.

"Not sure. But I felt it coming a long time ago. He wasn't the same Windy this year."

"Why do you think he left?"

"He didn't say. Just told Cummins he was leaving, picked up his paycheck, and was gone."

"A month or two ago, he said something to me that didn't make too much sense. I forgot about it till now," Bud said.

Dough looked at him questioningly.

Bud paraphrased what Windy had said, being there six years, having all the girls he wanted with no responsibilities, what a great life it was, and what a waste.

Dough silently nodded, he understood, keeping his attention on the game. "Waste. Maybe he's right," he said moments later.

"Do you think it's a waste?"

Dough stared vacantly at the TV. When he started guarding years ago, he never thought it would be his life. But the years passed, the inclination to leave receded, and it became easier and easier to slide with the tide. He had no responsibility except to himself. He did what he wanted when he wanted. There were many perks. Joining the Army was one. His MOS—Military Occupational Specialty—was Special Services, which included being a lifeguard at the base swimming pool. His whole platoon was wasted in Nam while he sat at the post swimming pool watching after officers' wives and kids. The kids were no problem. The wives were. He'd seen many an officer's bedroom in his two years as lifeguard. He got used to the lifestyle of no responsibility. For him, the Army was a holiday.

By the time he married Pat, he was used to the easy living, good pay, and leisure time. His son, Cal, was born. Lifeguarding was the perfect job. Pat waitressed part time at the local bar. They were always together. Their rented house a few blocks from the Santa Monica beach was always full, laughter and happiness flourished. But as Cal grew, expenses grew. Pat's attitude changed. She'd asked Dough to finish college so he could get a better job. His pride was hurt by her insinuation. Plus, he liked the all-night partying and the endless succession of surfing trips he and his buddies took going to Mexico or Hawaii for a surfing contest. They were making good money under the circumstances. If they tightened their belts, they could make it. He'd taken the job in Lauderdale for just that reason. It was cheaper to live in Lauderdale and there was a good chance of promotion. The promotion to supervisor took longer than expected and Pat was unhappy. She'd often told him he was wasting his life. He could do better than being a lifeguard, and they weren't getting any younger. They couldn't go on partying, not thinking of the future. They had Cal to think about.

Bud's question brought it all back. He saw himself in Bud, fifteen years earlier. The future ahead of him, but that future had passed. He was now almost forty and had gone as far as he could. All positions in the upper echelons of the Parks Department required a college degree. Windy was right. It was a waste. Pat was right. He'd wasted his earlier years and his life. He was reluctant to admit it. He had no place to go, except where he was.

"I don't know if it's a waste," Dough said. "But if I had it to do all over again, I'd think twice." It was the closest he'd go to admitting he was a failure.

"What do you mean? "Bud asked.

Why the hell doesn't he stop with the questions? Does he think they can be answered with one-liners? One word? "What do you mean? "Dough repeated, in a whisper to himself.

Bud envied Dough. He wanted to be like him. Dough had found his place. He was happy. He'd amounted to something. He wasn't a beach bum like the others. He was a supervisor. Bud naively thought Dough was successful and happy.

This kid has no idea of the banal life he'd led. He wished he'd never heard of lifeguarding. If Bud could see inside Dough's head, he'd know Dough was more confused than he was himself. Not only did he not have answers to Bud's questions, but he also wished Bud had never asked them. He didn't want the responsibility. He'd mapped out his life so he wouldn't have responsibility, and he didn't want to be responsible for anyone. He tried like hell to dissuade kids like Bud from becoming guards. He gave the hardest tests. The two kids who took the test with Bud months ago would never know that it was he who didn't pass them. Cummins was unaware that Dough was the main reason they were always short of guards. He talked disparagingly about life on the beach. He had to restrain himself from coming right out and telling them to get back home before they wasted their lives, that there was no future in lifeguarding, that if they stayed, they were giving up more than their youth. They were giving up their lives.

He saw it in Windy six years ago, a fresh-faced kid right out of high school, fearing the draft, trying to outrun it if it came his way. It was in his eyes, in his demeanor. Nothing Dough said could dissuade Windy. He wanted to be a lifeguard. If Dough didn't give him a chance, he would try Palm Beach or Key West. He wanted Lauderdale, but if he had to split, he would go somewhere else. Dough knew that Windy was a born beach bum. There was nothing he could do but give the hardest test he could and hope he'd fail, discourage him from trying anywhere else. If he passed, at least he'd be able to watch him, as he had done with Bud. He'd lost his son and wife, and now he was guardian to all the guards. He was the surrogate father of the beach bums.

How could he tell this callow kid sitting in front of him all that and hope he believed him? He wasn't that strong to accept that kind of responsibility. He never was. He didn't mind watching out for his guards, but he didn't want the responsibility of changing the course of their lives. He was glad Windy had taken off. Maybe the draft finally caught up to him? But Dough was angry that Windy had held up the mirror of failure and his life was reflected there. Before he knew what he was doing, he was on his feet, standing over Bud.

"Get the hell out of here. Don't come around with your stupid fucking questions. If you need help, go to a priest or a shrink. But don't come to me," Dough bellowed.

Bud was stunned. He was afraid Dough was going to hit him.

"I didn't ..." Bud started to say.

"I don't want to hear any more of your fucking shit," Dough cut in, advancing toward him. "Just get the hell out of here." He pulled the door open so hard, it shook on its hinges.

Bud cautiously moved past Dough on the way out, confused by Dough's behavior. On the way to The Box, he naively put it down to Windy leaving, causing major changes in the lifeguard schedule. He too would be pissed off if he were in charge and one of his senior guards just took off without notice.

***

A light drizzle had started, dark clouds casting the beach in shadow. The Box was full, the beach bums already gearing up for a night on the town. Bud waved hello on the way up to the apartment. He showered and changed. The night was just starting.

The Shack was as crowded as ever. Bob was behind the bar. Bud and Bev made their way to a makeshift table made out of an old telephone cable reel. Max was there drinking a beer. The jukebox was deafening. Dim lighting lit the interior. Shadows danced on the walls.

The beer was flowing. Conversation was drowned out by loud music. Windy leaving was never mentioned. No one needed a reminder of their nihilistic life.

Bud reached in his pocket and came up empty. Bev handed him a few dollars for a round of drinks. As he was paying, he was accidentally pushed by someone, but took no notice. Bud had lost all track of time, drink and tiredness settling in. He put his head on Bev's shoulder. New faces came in and out of focus; one or two looked familiar. Someone was arguing with Mike. The argument got louder. Mike looked over at Max. A silent communication passed between them. Something wasn't right. The hair on Max's neck bristled.

Max noticed the new faces gathering at the bar. Mike came over. "I think there's going to be trouble. Bud threw a punch at one of these guys," Mike said. It was the same guy Max told to leave The Box weeks before. Mike finished his beer, suggesting to the others it was time to go.

"Hey buddy, got a quarter?" the kid asked Max loudly.

Max shook his head and said, "No."

"Come on, put some money in," the kid told him.

Max tapped Bud. "Let's go," he said.

Bud finished his beer. There was a loud scuffle going on behind him. He turned and Max was on the floor. Three young, muscular T-shirted guys were kicking him. He saw someone lifting a stool and crashing it down on the bar, missing Bob by inches. Within seconds, The Shack was turned into a free-for-all. Bud dived at the three hippos kicking Max. He hit them with his shoulder, knocking them off balance. As if instilled with the strength of ten, he held them firm against the wall. They lashed out in a flurry of wild punches. Bev's voice cut through the fray, "Bud. Bud," then he heard the crash of a chair and the smash of bottles. He held his two prizes with vice-like strength. Their continued punches on Bud's back started to have an effect, weakening his grip.

Mike moved just in time to miss the whizzing stool that crashed into the jukebox, breaking the glass and stopping the music with a shrill scratch as the needle scraped across the record. He turned instinctively, putting a fist into his assailant's face. Blood splattered from his mouth and nose. Max was up defending himself against the three who had now multiplied into ten. They were all over, hitting anyone. The girls were screaming. Bud was finally pummeled into releasing his hold. He ducked just as a fist came in his direction. Grabbing his assailant by the legs, he toppled him over, cracking his head on the cement floor. He lay motionless, bleeding. With the rage and hate of a killer, he was up, coming for Bud. Luckily, another of the kids jumped on Bud and started pounding him with powerful punches. The bloody assailant who was after him dove past, hitting the door, crashing through onto the street.

"Bud, get out of there. Get out!" Bev's voice cut through the uproar. He was being attacked by two more. Bev's hands were covering her face in fear. Bud moved as if shot out of a cannon, colliding with them, driving them straight to the back wall. A chair flew through the air, smashing the new window Bob had just put in. Glass showered down on Bud. He scrambled away, shouting to Bev, "Get the hell out of here! Get out!"

Max and Bob were fighting off six. The fight was carried out to the street. Bodies were cut and bleeding. In the distance, a siren broke through the night. The kids scrambled into a pickup truck and took off. Bob and Max took off after them. The others watched as they disappeared into the night. The girls were comforting their friends, tears streaming down their faces.

"Let me look at you," Bev said, concerned.

"I'm okay," Bud replied, making light of it.

They went back into The Shack. Broken tables and chairs were all over. A stool was sticking out of the jukebox. Jagged bottles oozing liquid littered the floor. Windows were shattered, letting the humid air of the night whistle through. The carnage would be remembered. Bev was shocked at the devastation. They started straightening up. Ann unconsciously said out loud, "Good God, what a mess."

A car pulled up outside. A young police officer came in. "They're on their way to the police station. Got them on US 1."

Bud led Bev outside. Bob would have to hire help to put his place back into shape. They had done all they could. He headed toward the police station.

"There it is," Bev pointed to the one-story Dania police station.

He pulled up alongside the pickup truck the kids had used trying to escape. The crest of Florida was etched in the marble they walked over going into the station. Bob and Max were talking to three cops.

In one corner was a holding cell with the kids, all smirking, their inebriated antagonism evident. One of the cops opened the cell door, beckoned one out. Like a bolt of lightning, three took off through the door, pushing the cop away and knocking Bud and Bev against the wall.

"Those bastards!" the cops yelled, racing after them.

Max, Bob, and Bud followed. The other cops grabbed their weapons and took up the chase. The cell door was closed by one on the way out. The police station erupted into a frenzy. Cops appeared from out of nowhere. Some jumped into cruisers and sped out of the parking lot. Others gave chase on foot.

The three kids were running for their lives, jumping cars, bushes, anything that got in their way. The cops called for them to stop. They didn't. Guns were drawn. One of the kids fell as he rounded a corner. In an instant he was up running again. Bud and Max gave chase. The cops, and Bob, headed in another direction.

"They went over the wall!" Max yelled. "You go over, I'll go left."

Bud jumped, grabbed the top of the wooden fence, and hoisted himself over like an Olympic athlete, landing on his feet. Near a toolshed in the yard, Max was punching one of the kids he'd caught. Blood instantly appeared from his mouth and he went down in pain.

"In the shed!" Max yelled to Bud. He grabbed the kid by the collar dragging him to his feet, holding him off the ground like a rag doll.

"We have your buddy big shot!" Max yelled.

Bud approached the shed cautiously. He kicked the door open, stepped out of the line of fire, just in case. The kid was curled up on the floor holding his leg.

"My leg's broken," he cried in anguish.

"Crawl, fuck," Max ordered.

Bud helped him to his feet. His right leg was hanging limp. His face full of pain.

"You stupid fucking bastards," Max said, full of malice. "You're lucky you're not dead." He started dragging them away.

The Slow Wave

Bob opened the station door. Max pushed the kids in. The injured one fell on his leg, crying out in agony.

"Get in there with your buddies," one of the cops ordered, holding his gun at the ready.

The injured kid was helped by his buddy into the cell. His friends gathered round him protectively, their faces now filled with sober fear.

"Where's the other one?" the cop asked.

"Here he is," came the answer. Standing in the door was the other kid, blood spilling from his nose and mouth.

Bev turned away, getting sick.

"In there with your friends, friend," said the arresting cop, pushing him toward the holding cell. "He fell over a garbage can," he said to his colleagues, knowing smiles covering their faces.

Five cigarettes later, Bud was still waiting to make his report and identification. Of the ten in the cell, nine were under twenty-one, one had false ID; four of them were in college, and four others were due to go in the Army the following week, if they weren't in jail. Two others were still in high school. Bud was told their arraignment would be on Friday at eight in the morning. He and Bev left, exhausted.

The sun was coming up. A new day was dawning on Ft. Lauderdale.

- 28 -

"I can't move my leg," Bud said, trying to get out of bed.

Bev knelt beside him, lifting the covers. "Oh my God," she cried. Bud's buttocks and upper thigh were a deep indigo.

"Where the hell did that come from?" he said.

He tried getting up, but the pain shot through him like a knife. He lay back, his back throbbing in short bursts of pain.

"Oh shit," he said through clenched teeth.

"You can't go to work," Bev said. "Get someone to cover for you."

"This is all I need. Cummins hears about this and I'm out."

"It wasn't your fault. He can't."

"Yes he can. That night in jail almost did it. I'll have to make it, even if I just sit out the day," he said.

"Let me call Dough. Maybe he can help."

"No! He can't do anything!" Bud shouted, the memory of what happened at Dough's apartment vivid.

"But …" Bev started.

"I said no!" he shouted. "Now get the hell out of the way."

Bev stepped back, shocked. She never expected such an outburst from Bud. It was terrifying.

He wrenched in pain every time he moved. She went to help. His eyes met hers with such distain she backed away. This was another person in front of her.

For the past few weeks, Bud had been edgy. He was settling into a way of life that she felt he distrusted, but that was consuming him. What they had, love and compassion, was ending. Making love and feeling his warmth against her made her forgive his transgressions, which she knew were frequent. The nights sleeping around had increased. She knew what he was doing. Ft. Lauderdale was a small town. There were no secrets, especially between the beach bums. She had grown to love him. Although she was part of the beach crowd, at the same time she wasn't. She guarded her privacy, wasn't promiscuous, and maintained an aloofness that was accepted by the beach crowd. Bud was endangering that. His philandering behavior was demeaning her.

Bud was sitting up on the edge of the bed, bathed in pain. He inched his body upright, hunched over like an invalid alleviating some of the pain. He agonizingly straightened his body. Taking baby steps to the bathroom, he splashed water on his face and brushed his teeth, then carefully, he put on his bathing trunks. The pain excruciating. Never once looking at Bev. He felt embarrassed, inadequate, stupid. Apprehension engulfed him. His job in the balance. He had to make it through the day.

He slowly ambled out of the apartment, cautiously drove to station 7, took his gear from his car, and prepared for the day. He pulled himself onto the stand, settling into as comfortable a position as he could. The pain was extant. The slightest move caused a jarring pain to shoot through him. His entire left side felt like a pin cushion.

The beach was deserted; only two adventurous people tested the surf, the torrential downpour last night keeping people away. As the weather cleared, he knew the beach would fill. Hopefully, there would be no incidents. Something must have happened to his vertebrae. He could feel it swelling as the morning passed. His bathing suit felt like a second skin, it was so tight. He wondered if he may have to cut it off. If the pain continued, there would be no alternative. He couldn't see himself pulling and tugging while the pain overwhelmed him. None of the beach crowd showed. He was alone, something he thought would never happen. The only people he could see were the lifeguards at their stations to his left and right.

Bud had overheard the kid who started the fight talking to the cops. At the time, he didn't pay it much attention. The kid had been watching every place on the beach the beach bums frequented, The Shack, The Box, and Omar's trying to catch them at a disadvantage—drunk. The stupid kid held a grudge for two months until it festered into retaliation. Along with some buddies, he chose last night to settle the score.

Bud didn't leave for lunch. He was in too much pain. He just shifted his position every few minutes to ease the pain, impatiently waiting for the day to end. He saw Bev going into The Box and waved. She waved back, smiling. Maybe things weren't as bad as she thought. The beach started to fill. Unfortunately, Tony was among the first to show up.

"Hey, I heard what happened," he said. "Hope no one was hurt."

Bud laughed. "Well, there was one. Me."

"You're bullshitting?"

"It feels like my back is broken. I can hardly move," Bud said.

"You look okay," Tony said, smirking. "You're bullshitting."

"What do you call this?" Bud turned his back to Tony.

"Shit man, you'd better see a doctor. That looks terrible."

"I'll be alright. It's just black and blue," Bud said, not really believing himself.

"Who started it?"

"It was the same kid Max and I had a run in with a couple of months ago. Remember?"

"I wish I was there. I haven't had a good fight in a long time," Tony said, with bravado. "I'll see you around. I'm off to Palm Springs."

The beach crowd descended as usual when the sun broke through. They'd all heard about the fight. Could it be the same bunch who started a big beach brawl last year? Bud didn't know. His friends advised him to see a doctor. If a doctor told him he couldn't work, what would Cummins say? Could he justify the actions of last night? He wasn't sure.

When his shift ended, he slowly shuffled across the street, relieved that the day was over. He was surprised that he had endured a full shift. There were a few moments during the day when he thought he wouldn't make it. He stowed his gear and went upstairs, falling onto the couch in agony.

- 29 -

Bright sunlight woke him. Bev was still sleeping. He inched up, the pain still there. He made his way to the bathroom. The discoloration had spread to the whole of his back. Slowly, he moved to the kitchen, put on water for coffee. He brought his coffee to the bed.

Bev stirred, rolled over, blinking from the bright sunlight.

"How do you feel?" she asked.

Bud shrugged but the expression on his face belied his true feelings. Bev got herself a cup of coffee, searching his eyes for communication. He looked away unable to say anything, but she had seen the worry in them. No one spoke. If he could make it through the day, he would be all right. He was off tomorrow. He wished himself luck and left.

Bev was wondering how long this would go on. Was it worth the aggro? She knew he was under pressure, that his job hung in the balance. Two months ago, he would have confided in her. Now they were like strangers. The destructive beach philosophy had gotten to Bud. What had made him change? The women? The drinking? The insouciant life? Had he become a nihilist like all the beach bums? She decided to ask. No matter what the consequence.

Beach activity was slow all morning. A few traffic wardens were giving out parking tickets. Pedestrian traffic was minimal. The place was deserted.

Bud was thinking, *What if I moved out?* He could always find another chick. That wasn't a worry. Marge, Judy, Anne, and maybe even Natalie, someone he'd met only last week. Any of them could take Bev's place. Although she was loving and kind, and afforded him a roof over his head, Bud was more independent since becoming a lifeguard, with a salary and friends. He was mistaking independence for ennui. He justified everything that happened to him since arriving: the fight, Dee, jail, Bev's support, indiscretions. This was his life now. He really believed what he was telling himself. The irrational justification made him conquer all his objections to his new decadent life.

He had a quick lunch at Mary's greasy spoon, the hamburger consumed in a few bites. Max came by and they went over the entire fight, concluding that Bud's injury must have been caused as he was protecting Bev, when the barstool that was thrown broke over Bud's back. Max had a few bruises but nothing to incapacitate him. He left, telling Bud he'd see him later at The Box.

Bud looked out over the panorama of water. So quiet. So vicious. What secrets it held. What secrets the beach held. Every section had a tale to tell. The section the beach bums made their home must have the bawdiest secrets. Every day he spent in Lauderdale made him a part of it. A consummate part of something. He had always wanted to belong, be part of something, and now he was. It didn't matter how crude or debauched. Forty-five minutes left to the end of his shift, then he would be off for forty-eight hours. Maybe he would see a doctor.

Something caught his eye. A volley of splashes about forty or fifty yards out. He grabbed the binoculars. A young girl was in trouble. He lowered himself slowly, pain shooting through him. He could hardly walk. Each step was like a blow to his body. When he reached the water, Mike came running down the beach shouting, "Get your torpedo and meet me in the water!" Mike hit the water in a perfect dive, racing toward the victim, his torpedo slung over his shoulder. Bud went back for his torpedo. He eased his way to the surf, but the undercurrent made him wrench in pain as he tried maintaining his balance.

Mike was yelling for him to get there. His legs were useless. He couldn't move and almost went under himself. The torpedo kept him afloat. Mike had the victim in a cross-chest carry. On the beach he administered CPR. After regaining her equilibrium, the look of relief and gratitude was plainly visible on her face.

"Thank you. I had cramps," she said, breathing naturally.

Mike eyed Bud, concern written there. He knew his report couldn't mention Bud. He would make it read as though the incident happened on his station.

The young girl gave her name and address to Mike for his report, then Mike walked her to her car parked on A1A. She thanked him again and left. Mike joined Bud at the stand.

"I'll say it happened on my station. Cummins won't question the report," Mike said.

"I couldn't make it. My legs wouldn't work," Bud said. He knew what would happen if Cummins found out the truth.

"I have to get my gear. See you later," Mike said and headed for his station.

Bud collected his gear and went to The Box for a beer. The aftermath of what he'd just gone through hit him. Although The Box was cool, he was sweating. The thought of what could have happened was frightening. He ignored Bev who was standing across from him on the other side of the bar. She could see he was upset. He looked up. What the hell is she looking at? *Can she tell I almost killed someone?* he wondered. *Is it that obvious?* He gulped his beer and hobbled out without saying anything.

Holy shit, I almost killed someone. He started crying in shame. A short time later, Bev came in and went straight into the shower, determined to stay out of his way. Hopefully in time he would say something. She made a cup of coffee, sat at the kitchen table, and continued drying her hair. Bud waited for her to say something. The image of the teenager floundering flashed into his head. He shivered in fear.

"I almost killed someone today," he said, solemnly.

It caught her off guard. She wasn't expecting this. She thought his first words would be about their argument earlier. "How?"

"I couldn't make it out to a swimmer. Mike had to run from his station and take over. I didn't even see her until she was almost gone," he said, remorse in every word.

"Then she's all right?" Bev said, trying to instill confidence.

"Yes, she's all right. But she could have drowned."

"But she's all right now," she said again, hoping to lighten his guilt.

Silence.

"I'll fix dinner," she said. "Or do you want to go somewhere?"

He ignored her and just stared up at the ceiling.

Bev went into the kitchen.

"No. Let's go out. I have to get away from here," he said.

Bev drove to Plantation and they had dinner in strained silence. He was still in shock, knowing he had almost caused someone's death. He couldn't find words to describe his feelings. Bev was reluctant to say anything, thinking it would cause another argument. Since they had been growing apart, she was aware that the slightest misspoken word would turn into an argument. She paid the bill. It made Bud feel worse.

On the drive back, Bev tried starting a conversation. Bud remained silent, lost in morbid thoughts of death.

Bud fell asleep in seconds. Bev lay awake, wondering what the future would bring.

***

Bev woke at twelve thirty, a bright sun shining through the windows. Bud still asleep. She gingerly crept around trying not to make noise.

The bright sun streaming through the blinds hit Bud across the eyes. He inched up on his elbows. Spying Bev, he smiled awkwardly. She handed him a cup of coffee. There was no trace of melancholy or morose. Sleep had acted as a solvent. Bud sipped his coffee, slowly.

"How do you feel?" she asked.

"Fine. Almost like new."

He slipped from under the covers and slowly got out of bed. The pain was still there, but bearable. He stood under the shower letting the hot water soothe him. He came out, a towel wrapped around him. They ate scrambled eggs and toast, while Bud told her what had happened. Bev hesitatingly kissed him, not sure if he would accept her touch. She wasn't sure it would be all forgotten in a few days but told him not to worry about it any longer. She wanted to say as little as possible, still not sure their relationship was redeemable.

The next two days were carefree, spent on the beach taking in the sun and gossiping with the beach bums. Mike said his report hadn't been questioned. Bud was relieved. His job was secure. Judy and Marge told them that Bob was going to sue the families of the kids who started the fight for damages. The nights were spent making love as if nothing inimical had passed between them.

- 30 -

He wasn't on the stand more than an hour when the phone rang. Cummins wanted to see him as soon as possible. Instant fear replaced calm. He put his gear in the car and drove through the still sleeping city, marshalling his thoughts to face Cummins.

"I was going over Mike's report," Cummins said, holding it up.

Bud was sure his pounding heart could be heard.

"It says here that Mike pulled the victim out at 4:48 at station 6, and that you assisted. I checked the schedule and Mike wasn't on station 6, but station 10. I just spoke to him and he says he switched with Jake. Now when Jake checked in at 4:45, Mike also checked in. He said that by the time he got back to station 6 the office would be closed. But his report says 4:48 rescue operation complete. Can you explain that?"

Bud's mouth was dry. Stuttering, he said, "I don't have any idea. It must be a mistake."

"If it is a mistake, it has to be straightened out. If Mike was not on his station when this occurred, he's liable for dismissal. Thanks heavens you were there and could prevent a serious accident." Cummins said.

Bud wasn't the one who was in trouble; it was Mike. In doctoring the report, Mike had put himself in jeopardy and mistakenly made Bud out to be a hero. Cummins dialed Mike's station and read the report to him. From Cummins's reaction, Bud could see he wasn't satisfied.

"You'd better get down here. This has to be straightened out," he said.

Cummins hung up. He told Bud to sit and wait. Within twenty minutes, Mike was standing alongside Bud.

"Now Mike, what time did all this happen? If it's a mistake, we'll just change it." Cummins said.

Mike explained that it was a mistake. That he'd written the wrong time down. What with not being at his station and checking out he'd made a mistake. He was sorry for the inconvenience.

"Okay, I'll accept that. An honest mistake. Next time make sure you get your reports correct," Cummins said. "That's all."

In the parking lot, Mike said, "What a dumbass. Why couldn't I just put 3:38? None of this would have happened. I'll see you later," he said.

"Right," Bud said.

"If it comes up again, just stick to the story."

"Okay. See you later."

Shadows were falling, with a sky dark and dull. Rain was in the air. The beach was almost empty. They had been lucky. But none of this would have happened if that girl had gone swimming further down the beach, better still if she hadn't gone swimming at all.

"Turner, Six," Bud said, grabbing the phone.

"Bud, I'm afraid you'll have to turn your gear in. I just spoke to Mr. Sylvester, the girl's father. He said the incident happened around five and that the lifeguard on duty couldn't even swim because of a bad limp. I already spoke to Jake and Mike. The three of you will be on suspension until I find out what really happened."

Bud put the receiver back, stunned. Now what? I just got three of us fired. *What the hell am I going to do?* he asked himself.

The sky held no sign of clearing as a light rain started to fall.

- 31 -

The next morning all three were standing in front of Cummins. He told them what he had found out. He wanted it straight from the horse's mouth. Bud related the entire incident. Cummins reinstated Jake and Mike. He told Bud to stay.

Cummins said he would have to let him go. He understood Jake's and Mike's loyalty and admired them for sticking by it. He was also glad to see that Bud had enough fortitude to tell him the truth. But the situation was serious, and he couldn't take the chance of it happening again or something more serious in the future. Bud listened to his own eulogy, depression settling in. Cummins had heard about the fight. If Bud would've come to him concerning the injury, he was quite sure something could've been worked out. He was sorry he had to dismiss Bud. There was nothing he could do under the circumstances.

Bud handed his gear in and drove to The Box in a state of shock. Bev gave him a beer. He told her what had happened, finished his beer, and had another, trying unsuccessfully to wash the incident away. She didn't know what to say to relieve his anxiety. She remembered the last time she tried giving advice.

He continued drinking all afternoon. By five o'clock he was drunk. When they left, he threw a five dollar bill on the counter. Bev picked it up when he turned away. He didn't remember paying already. They went upstairs. Bud fell into a deep, troubled sleep.

***

It was dark when Bud woke up. He reached for the clock; it read twelve thirty. He left Bev sleeping and went to Omar's. He had severance pay to spend. The place was packed. Marge, Delores, and Mike were at their usual table. They waved him over. He ordered a beer from the waitress as he made his way through the dancers and drinkers. Bud looked bleary-eyed at Mike and shrugged his shoulders, as if to say, oh well. Mike pursed his lips tightly in empathy. Bud's senses were dulled by drink. The music sounded far away. The people were all a blur. A moving indecipherable collage. Bud finished his beer and ordered another.

"Sorry to hear about it, Bud," Judy said.

Bud shrugged his shoulders. "That's okay," he slurred. They knew why he was drinking: depression and frustration at losing his job. It didn't happen often and when it did, it was usually to someone not as close to the beach bums as Bud had become. Mike was surprised he was even standing. He knew that if he had been fired, he wouldn't be able to talk, much less walk.

Others came by offering their condolences. At the same time inviting him to a big blow out next week, not really anticipating seeing him around much longer. Without the lifeguard job, there was nothing for him to stay in Lauderdale for. He waved a limp arm in thanks. "See you there," he said. Marge pulled him onto the dance floor. He was spastic, bouncing off everyone. Harsh criticism from fellow dancers had no effect. Marge steadied him, leading him back to the table. Minutes later the call for closing blared out from a bullhorn. The place cleared out slowly. The only ones remaining were the beach crowd. Mike suggested they get Bud back to Bev's. He lifted Bud out of the chair, walking him outside into the light rain that was falling.

The rain combined with the humidity created a thin mist over the beach. A surreal picture materialized as cars and pedestrians appeared to be coming out of a fog. Bud pushed Mike away and weaved in the direction of The Box. He hit the bench at the bus stop almost falling over. Marge and Judy ran to help, but he waved them away. They watched as he weaved his way up the street. Suddenly he darted across

A1A missing cars by inches on his way to the surf. The water covered him like a liquid blanket, submerging him without a trace. Buoyant as a cork he reappeared, floating on his back as if casually sunbathing.

The rain started coming down harder, hiding Bud behind a torrential wall. He stood on unsteady legs, then began jogging down the beach away from his friends who had followed him to the surf to make sure he was all right.

"I think we better get him out of here before he hurts himself. Or worse, drowns," Marge said.

"Okay," Jody said.

Mike and the girls caught up with him and lead him away from eventual calamity. He collapsed onto Mike's shoulders like a deflated balloon. By the time they reached Delores's and Marge's apartment, they were drenched to the skin.

***

Bud was still asleep at noon the next day. Marge had put a light blanket over his nude body after they had stripped him of his wet clothes and dried him. They guessed he'd sleep most of the day. He had consumed enough beer to float a small ship. They had hung his clothes in the sun to dry. When they were dry, Marge put them on the back of a chair, ready to be worn by their friend who had used his body as a liquor bottle.

Scotty was Bud's replacement at South 7. Dough went by The Box. Bev told him that Bud had not come home last night. She was sure nothing had happened to him or else they would have heard. His car was still out back.

Dough prowled the beach looking for a sleeping body. There were times when he was soused, he used the beach for a bed. He had been in Miami for the last two days attending a beach patrol supervisor meeting. When he heard what happened, he tried unsuccessfully to have Bud reinstated. Cummins was adamant. He wouldn't even let Dough take responsibility for Bud's future behavior. Arguing was futile. Dough at first was frustrated at not getting Bud's job back, then secretly glad. Bud would now have to leave Ft. Lauderdale, the wasted life of a beach bum no part of his future.

With all that happened, he would make Bud realize that Lauderdale was no place for him or anybody, except tourists, and that one day, Ft. Lauderdale would be tourist heaven and lifeguards would be an anachronism. In the years to come, the carefree days of now would be a distant memory. Lifeguarding would be turned into big business with BAs, business degrees, and PhDs necessary.

The meeting in Miami was the beginning. There was talk of how to eliminate the college binge mentality that infested Miami and Ft. Lauderdale. Big business was interested in these areas. There was no money in college students. The big bucks would be in tourism and real estate, and with that would come the change from fun-loving lifeguarding to career-minded beach personnel.

All the hopes and desires he once had for himself he wished for Bud. He didn't want to be responsible for another wasted life. This was his chance to make amends, to hopefully right all the wrongs of his past life, from his failed marriage and loss of his son to what he had become, a beach bum.

***

By three o'clock Bud was still missing. Word spread. Apprehension grew, followed by fear. The beach crowd started searching. Dough saw Lou, who told him that Bud had left with Mike, Marge, Delores, and Judy last night. He knew where Marge lived. He headed in that direction.

Delores answered the door dressed in a muumuu. Bud was asleep on the floor. She told him what happened after they left Omar's. Marge came out of the shower drying her hair, unaware that Dough was there. She casually excused herself and disappeared into the bedroom, coming out moments later dressed in a terry cloth robe.

"How long has he been asleep?" Dough asked, spying pieces of paper, crumpled bills, and a wallet on the table.

"Since about two," Marge said.

Delores handed him a cup of coffee.

Marge was sure Bud had spent a lot of money on booze and maybe even lost some taking a dip in the ocean. They'd emptied his pocket when they took his clothes off. His wallet held a few soggy pieces of paper. Marge handed them to Dough plus the crumpled money, a letter from his mother, unreadable. The other papers were mangled, including his driver's license. He put them on the table. He would be back in two hours. Bud should be awake by then. He went to tell Bev he'd found Bud. She thanked him without enthusiasm. Dough felt the estrangement immediately.

He was back at Marge's by five o'clock. Bud was just waking up, moving slowly like a baby crawling for the first time. Dough helped him into the shower holding him under the ice cold water, shocking him out of his stupor. His head felt like a kettle drum, still pounding lightly. He said he could manage by himself. Dough took his clothes from the chair and put them on the toilet seat. A few moments later, Bud came out. He didn't remember anything. Marge handed him a cup of coffee then told him of last night's events. He was numb with shock. The last thing he remembered was having a beer at The Box. Everything else was blank. Bud thanked the girls and left with Dough.

"I tried to get Cummins to reinstate you, but he said no. You should've told him what happened. He would have given you a few days off," Dough said, as they walked back to A1A.

"After the jail thing, I thought he'd fire me on the spot," Bud said.

"Why didn't you come to me? I would've covered for you."

Bud looked at him skeptically. As if Dough could read his mind, he told him that what he had said was out of frustration not anger at him. No matter, he should have still come over. They were friends.

Bud explained what happened, but Dough was unforgiving. He didn't understand why Bud took such a chance.

Bud would have to get another job. Where? He didn't know. There must be something around. He'd start looking tomorrow. Dough handed him back his wallet and letter. He ripped the letter into small pieces without remorse and threw it away. He looked despairingly at what remained of his salary: three crumpled ones and a five. He couldn't believe he spent all his money. Dough said he'd lend him some until he got back on his feet. Bud declined the offer, saying he had some at the apartment. Dough's parting advice was maybe Bud should think about leaving Ft. Lauderdale.

Bev was at the apartment waiting. He hugged her, sat on the couch, depressed. What was he going to do? He could get a job easily enough; the season was going to start at the end of the month. Where? What? Bartender. Short order cook. Waiter. He didn't know. He would make up his mind eventually. Whatever it was, it wouldn't be as convenient as beach patrol.

Bev sat next to him, waiting. Was now the time to confront him with their disintegrating relationship? When nothing was forthcoming, she went to the kitchen to put together something to eat. When he had something to say, he would say it.

They ate in silence. She would not force conversation. She knew what had happened. She wanted to hear it from Bud, to know if there was a future. The sound of the waves breaking on the beach across A1A made Bud think of all that he had lost. Bev felt the tension and cleared the table, wishing that Bud would speak to her. It surprised her when he said he was going out.

"I'd like to talk," she said, before he opened the door.

"About what?" he asked.

"About us."

He sat on the couch, glancing out over the water. Bev was nervous; she needed a cigarette, something to calm her. This wasn't the way she wanted it, but if it had to be this way, let it be.

"Do you think it's worth it? Do we have a future?" she calmly asked.

He repeated the questions, "Is it worth it? Do we have a future?" Then in a dull monotone, he added, "If I knew the answer to that, I'd know the answer to many things."

Bev knew she had cut deep. It was painful watching him. He was so confused.

"I've asked myself those same questions many times," Bud continued. "Each time I get the same answer. What is worth it? What future do we have?"

He lit a cigarette, contemplating the vast darkness in him. *What's the answer?* he wondered. *Is there an answer? Do I know the answer?* He looked across into two soulful eyes begging for something other than enigma.

"I'm not sure. I don't know what's expected of me. I don't think I've ever known," he said.

"We can't continue like this. My insides are turning to putty. I don't make sense to myself. I thought we had something substantial. I thought we had something," she said, hurting with each word.

Bud tried to suppress a laugh, but it grew into full self-mockery. "I can't make sense to myself," he said through a maniacal laugh that scared her. "I can't make sense to myself!" he screamed.

Bev was looking at a person she'd never met. His stare was vacant, as if drugged, and he was shaking. It wasn't what she expected. She didn't know what she expected, but she didn't expect this. A person she thought she knew and loved was now visibly falling apart in front her. He hugged himself viciously, as if trying to exorcise demons as tears burst from his eyes. She ran to him, wanting to protect him, cradle him, love him.

He rebuffed her, screaming that he didn't want her near him. "Stay away. Leave me alone. Don't touch me. You don't understand what's wrong. Leave me alone."

"I do know!" she screamed back. "I know. And I understand. I understand you wanting to get away from your family, wanting to get away from commitment, wanting to get away from boredom and responsibility. But don't blame me. I'm not the cause of your frustration, your insecurity. But I want to help. I want to be part of it. I'm not just a roommate, a casual fuck, or another summer fling. If I didn't feel all this was worth it, do you think I would've put myself in this position? Do you? I thought we had something. I thought we *were* something. I thought we were lasting. Tell me if we are," Bev said, staring him down, waiting for an answer.

Her words hit their mark. He was incapable of commitment. Incapable.

"This isn't pity. I'm not trying to pity you. I'm trying to love you. Do you know the difference?" she asked.

What happened? What had he done wrong again? Had he done the same thing with Shelia? With his father? Had he been wrong all his life? Why couldn't he see what was so obvious? She really did love him, and he was sure there was love back home. But there was no love in him. He didn't know what it meant. How does a person find out? Know? Learn? Questions. One after the other. Confusing questions he didn't have answers for. This was unbearable. He couldn't take it anymore. He reached for the doorknob.

"Don't go," she pleaded, looking into unresponsive eyes. "Please don't go."

He felt as if the ground was swallowing him. He wouldn't let himself look at her, afraid he would take her in his arms and beg forgiveness. He wouldn't let that happen. He wanted his freedom. He needed his freedom. If he stayed he knew it would never be the same, and he knew it would never be better. It never entered his mind that he could be wrong. That everything he needed was standing in front of him. He opened the door and walked out. He needed a drink. The Shack was just the place.

- 32 -

The Shack was empty. None of the beach crowd were around. After a few beers, Bud left. He took a drive to settle his nerves. He went through every charge over and over again: hangover on duty, incapacitation on duty, mendacity on duty, and the most serious, almost causing the death of a young swimmer. His depression deepened. He stopped at the bowling alley in Dania and had a few more drinks. He'd started with beer and progressed to Scotch. He was drowsy by the time he left. It started to rain. The top was down on the MG. The rain drenched him and the car. He passed The Box heading for Act One.

"Scotch," he mumbled. His vision was blurred, like looking through an unfocused lens. He finished his Scotch, ordered another. Someone put a hand on his shoulder. He turned to stare into Natalie's lovely face framed by the lights behind her on the wall.

"Hi," she said.

Bud saluted her with his glass. "Hi. Want a drink?" he said pointing to his Scotch.

She nodded. "Beer."

"One beer, if you please," he said.

"Heard you slept the whole day," she said.

"Yep, could've stayed right there too."

Natalie sipped her beer. Bud ordered another Scotch and hung his arm over her shoulder. She let it remain, liking the warmth of his body next to hers. They finished their drinks. Natalie suggested they leave. Bud dropped a few bills on the counter, and they jumped into Natalie's new T-Bird.

Bud was already half asleep. He put his aching head back, exhausted. Natalie was talking. Occasionally, he would utter "ah ha" and "yes." It was almost eleven thirty and the moon had come out after the rain stopped. She made a U-turn and drove home.

"We're here. Wake up. Wake up," she prodded, giving Bud a gentle shove.

He stirred, came out of a deep sleep, recognized Nat's smiling face, and leaned over, kissing her hard on the lips.

"Let's go in. Come on." Pulling him by the arm, she led him up the path to a white bungalow that sat quietly on the inward waterway off Bay View Drive.

She opened the door onto a large expansive living room. Bud flopped down on one of the three sofas arranged in an open three-sided square in the middle of the room. She took his flip-flops off, put his head on a cushion, brought a duvet from her bedroom and laid it over him, making sure he was comfortable. She secured the sliding glass doors leading to the wharf, where a fifty-two-foot cabin cruiser lay berthed, returned to her bedroom, and fell on the king-size bed with a self-pleasing smile on her face.

She had wanted to fuck Bud ever since she first laid eyes on him. She remembered the times they had danced, how his powerful body felt as it pressed up against hers, how his strong hands made her feel like clay when he put them on her. She knew some day her chance would come. Nobody stays with one person for too long on the beach. If you happened to get seconds, so be it. She was certain that if she had seen him first, she would have had him before Bev.

She was twenty-two and had been choosing her men since she was fifteen. Her wealth and independence were her strength. It was her parents' house and she used it all year. Her parents lived in Newport, Rhode Island, and only came down for the season. Half the year, she lived in the sumptuous white house by herself.

She had patiently waited for Bud to become her lover. She tingled with anticipation at the thought of him sleeping in the living room. Tomorrow she would fuck the life out of him. They would spend the whole day together on her father's cruiser. She'd been skippering boats since her early teens. She didn't want him seeing Bev or any of the beach crowd and feeling remorse. His dependence on her was the first step in her control. She wouldn't even let him collect his clothes. If he needed anything else, he could use some of her father's extensive wardrobe. This was Ft. Lauderdale, simple dress code, flip-flops, T-shirts, and bathing suits.

The cat with the purr of a kitten but the bite of a scorpion fell asleep on her down pillow knowing it would be Bud's resting place for the near future.

- 33 -

Blinking eyes looked through sliding glass doors onto beautiful, manicured grass that led to a luxurious cabin cruiser moored at the dock at the end of the fifty-foot lawn. He had no recollection of where he was. He sat up cautiously, not wanting to cause any more pain in his throbbing head than was already there. He tried in vain to recall the previous night. He toured the rooms off the living room. This was luxury he'd never experienced. Where was he? How the hell did he get here? Back in the living room, he sat on the couch holding his head between his legs trying to isolate the rumbling going on inside.

"You're up."

He looked up. Natalie, wearing tapered tan slacks, a flowered blouse, and sandals, was standing there.

She set a cup of coffee on the glass-topped table in front of Bud. "I'm surprised to see you up so early," she said, sitting next to him.

"I may be up, but my head doesn't know it," he said. "How did I get here? And where am I?"

"We're in my house. Or should I say, my parents' house."

Bud gave out a long slow whistle. "It looks like a palace, not a house."

"My parents live in Newport. I live here. It's a great arrangement. Let's have something to eat. Then you can hear the whole story of what happened last night."

Bud took a quick shower in a bathroom large enough for a dinner party, brushed his teeth with a brand-new toothbrush still packaged, and with a note saying "use this" resting on the side of one of the two marble sinks under a wall mirror encircled with theatrical lights, and slipped on his swim trunks and T-shirt. He joined Natalie in the kitchen where she prepared eggs, toast, and fresh coffee. She told him she'd caught up with him at Act One. He could pick up his car later or leave it until tomorrow or whenever. She'd made plans to take the cabin cruiser out for the day.

***

She gave Bud a pair of Top Sider deck shoes and moved the yacht through the Intracoastal Waterway and into a lagoon bordering the inlet to the ocean like an expert. He sat in a deck chair letting the hot sun beat down on his already suntanned body. Natalie idled the yacht joining others already there, and joined him.

"Boy, this is beautiful," he said, contentedly. "How come I never heard about all this luxury before?"

"Would it have made any difference?" she asked, coyly.

Bud squinted to keep the sun out of his eyes. It was a rhetorical question. He remained silent. One point for her.

The lagoon was calm. Schools of fish were swimming portside. Fishing boats were on their way back from an early morning run, flags hanging from masts signaling their catch. The coast looked beautiful. A white belt of beach stretched for miles along a narrow outline of rolling hills and estates. The yacht bobbed gently on the water. Natalie brought 7 Ups and ham sandwiches out, and they passed the afternoon relaxing and talking about nothing in particular. The sun was setting. Natalie headed the yacht back home. She kept the throttle steady and within an hour, they were moored and sitting in the living room, drinking champagne.

They ate on the patio overlooking the lights on the yacht, which she had left on. Bud was overwhelmed by all the grandeur. Natalie told him she had moved to Florida after a big snowstorm in Newport and never went back again. "All that cold. Who needs it?" All her education had been in private Southern girls' schools. Lauderdale had been her playground since her early teens.

Bud told her his familial history.

Although disinterested, she listened attentively. She had what she wanted. She was waiting for the right moment to experience it. "Would you get the cigarettes? They're on the counter in the kitchen near the freezer."

"Sure."

He returned with two packs of Marlboros. They pushed the dishes aside, lit cigarettes, and sat back listening to soft music coming from the hi-fi.

Bud remembered Natalie from the beach and how much different she was now. On the beach, she was the typical beach bum, idlily sunning herself and joining in the frivolity without any direction or opinions. Whatever was suggested, she enthusiastically joined in. Here, she had an air of authority and self-assuredness he hadn't noticed that was almost overwhelming. The carriage clock on the mantel read one o'clock.

"I better go. It's late," he said.

"That's okay. Stay," she purred.

She was inviting, with a Cheshire smile waiting for him to make a move. He kissed her on the lips. She drew him closer and returned his kiss passionately.

Lowering herself alongside him, she continued kissing him. He explored the sweetness of her body. She ran her hands through his hair and forced his face into her amble breasts. Passion swept through him. He cupped her breasts and felt their firmness. She purred reacting to every touch. He could feel the ridge of her pubis against his stiffened penis. He undid her blouse. She was braless. She pulled his T-shirt over his head and in the same motion swept away her blouse. Her hardened nipples pressed into his muscular chest. His excitement was uncontrollable. He had been thinking of making love to her all day.

This was the culmination of that desire. She responded in kind. She led him inside to her bed and together they released their passion. She cried out shrilly in heightened climax, her fingers tearing into his back, drawing lines of blood. It was the most exciting lovemaking he'd ever experienced.

- 34 -

For the next two weeks, they kept to the same schedule: making love, yachting, making love. They were insatiable. Natalie was certain there was no need to worry any longer about Bev.

"I'll drive you to your car. Follow me back," Natalie said.

She drove him to Act One. The seats of his car were damp from the periodic rain. He folded a towel into fours to sit on, then followed her back to the house. She prepared chicken wings, baked potatoes, and salad. A bottle of white wine sat in a glass cooler in the middle of the dining room table.

Bud left the house by himself for the first time the next day. He knew Bev would be at work when he collected his things. He parked in back of The Box, threw all his things in his carryall, and left the apartment key on the table.

***

Natalie showed him a closet off the master bedroom. "Travel light, don't you?" she said.

"All I need is a bathing suit. Clothes down here are taboo."

"Not where I'm concerned. Tonight some friends are having a party. I think you'll need a tie. Have one?" She leaned over and kissed him on the cheek, smiling to herself.

He pulled the only one he had out from under his sports jacket. She raised her eyebrows as if to say, you're kidding.

"What's wrong with it?" he asked.

"Nothing, if you're going to a masquerade party," she said, mockingly.

He looked at the tie with a newfound inquisitiveness. The little red designs dotted all over were outlined by white circles on a deep blue background. He didn't see anything wrong with it. Clothes were never a problem for him. If they fit, he wore them.

"What do you mean?"

"It's too busy. All those colors look terrible. You can use one of father's. He has dozens."

"Okay," he said. It didn't matter to him.

In the living room she asked him to fix her a gin and tonic while she went to change into a bathing suit. They would spend the day on the beach, then go to the party. She was sure of her position: Bud was hers now, for as long as she wanted.

There was a fully stocked wet bar in one corner of the room. He poured himself a small Black Label straight up and made Natalie her gin and tonic with a twist of lemon and ice he found in the small fridge under the service counter.

Natalie came back wearing a bikini. The dark tan of her perfect body gave new meaning to the word voluptuous, along with the two pieces of string vainly trying to hide her opulent assets. Ignoring her drink, she headed for the carport, tossing a matching see-through top over her arm and setting her sunglasses on top of her head.

Bud followed, letting the untouched drinks sit on the counter. He felt the seats of his MG. They were finally dry. It had taken more than a week for them to dry out.

He parked near The Box and they settled on the beach not far from station 7. Delores and Marge were there with Tony, who stopped in mid-conversation when they approached. Bud didn't notice the curious looks Natalie was getting from Delores and Marge. They knew that if Bud was on the beach with Natalie in broad daylight, he and Bev were no longer together. There had been rumors to that effect for the last few weeks. It happened all the time with the beach crowd. No need for verbal confirmation. Their presence together was sufficient.

"Boy, what a time we had," Tony continued on from what he was originally saying. "We hit every party going in Palm Beach. That chick knew everyone."

"You always find them," Bud said. "How do you do it?"

"Are you kidding? They're all over the place. A guy could die from all this physical exertion," he said laughing. "How's the back?"

"Almost back to normal," Bud said.

"It doesn't seem to be stopping you." Tony winked.

"We're going to The Shack tonight," Marge told him. "Bob has it all back together. First drink on the house."

Bud looked over at Natalie for confirmation. She remained expressionless. "I don't know. We have something to do. If we have time, we'll be there."

"Everyone's going to be there," Delores said.

"Come on, let's take a swim," Tony said.

"You go, I don't want to get my hair wet," Natalie said.

Everyone ran into the surf. Natalie closed her eyes to the sun and everything around her.

- 35 -

"Here, try this." Natalie gave Bud a beige medallion pattern Countess Mara tie. His clothes needed pressing but would pass for tonight. The tie matched perfectly. His loafers could use a shine. She would amend that in the future.

It was the first time Bud had worn anything but a bathing suit since coming to Ft. Lauderdale. It felt strange.

Natalie was wearing an elegant Yves Saint Laurent dress. Her hair was swept back, falling over her bare shoulders. A single strand of pearls round her neck. Bud was proud she was his date. He had never seen anyone from the beach crowd dressed so elegantly. Natalie had something none of the others had: sophistication and class.

They took Natalie's car to keep her hair from disarray.

"I need gas," she said.

He pulled into a Phillips 66.

"Fill it with high test," she said. "Here." She handed him twenty dollars.

The attendant cleaned the windshield and handed Bud the change.

"Keep it. My purse is too small for all those bills."

Bud stuffed the change in his jacket pocket. Natalie directed him past Sunrise and onto Oakland. He sped past The Chateau and down US 1.

***

"Take a right here," she said.

The sign read, "Coral Ridge Golf Course, two miles." He drove up to a sumptuous house off the first tee and parked alongside a Mercedes

SL 300, two brand new T-Birds, and a Porsche. He tried not to show his eagerness. Natalie led the way. At the front door, she straightened his tie.

"You look very handsome," she said, and kissed him lightly on the lips.

She pulled the door knocker back once. It struck like a kettle drum. The door was opened by a beautiful girl about the same age as Natalie. Her long, flowing blonde hair cascaded over her shoulders like a blanket. She was dressed in a one-piece black sheath dress. Her pearl necklace had three strands.

"Nat! What a surprise. I didn't think you'd make it," she said excitedly.

"This is Bud," Natalie said, stepping inside.

"Jackie. Nice to meet you."

Bud missed the nod Jackie gave Natalie. "Nice," she whispered as they walked into the living room. Natalie winked back. She knew Bud was something special. It made her happy her friends knew it also.

There were eight couples already drinking and talking. Jackie handed Bud a flute of champagne and introduced him. He was greeted with feigned politeness and left on his own.

"Now that we're all here, let's go in to dinner," she said.

Although Natalie sat alongside him, he felt awkward and alone. Already on the table was the first course, jellied consume and cream cheese with a caviar topping, which was a first for Bud. They went to a sideboard for their main course: roast leg of lamb sliced as thin as paper, baby potatoes, and string beans. Dessert was crème brûlée and espresso brought in by a liveried waitress. It was absolutely exquisite. He had never tasted food like it.

During the evening, he learned that Jackie had the same set up as Natalie, except that her parents lived in New York. A majority of the dinner guests lived in Palm Beach. They were rich and lived off their parents. They had finished college, but none had permanent jobs. Some worked for their parents' companies. They talked about jetting between the US and Europe.

Bud asked one of the girls from Palm Beach if she knew Tony Ellis, the show-off he knew from the beach.

"Yes. He was up two days ago," she said and promptly returned to her previous conversation.

Natalie was smiling to herself, aware of how awkward this was for Bud. It didn't matter to her. She could care less if he didn't get along with these people. It was a feather in her cap to show off such an attractive man to her stolid friends. Secretly, she knew all the girls at the table envied her.

Someone suggested The Chateau for after dinner drinks and dancing. Bud whispered in Natalie's ear that he didn't have enough money to go.

"Don't worry. I have a charge account there," she said.

Rick, the major domo, greeted Natalie and her friends effusively, ticking names off one after the other and showed the group to a large corner booth overlooking the city. He took their order and eyed Bud skeptically, more in surprise than disfavor. A small combo was playing Latin music. Couples went to dance. Bud had never noticed the view before, and he'd never been there so early. Every time he'd been, he was soused. They stayed until two thirty. As they were leaving, the beach crowd came in. Bud froze at seeing Bev. She ignored him and went immediately to the beach crowd's usual table. Bud introduced his new friends to the beach bums. The contrast between what the beach crowd was wearing—T-shirts and baggy pants—and what his new friends wore—suits, ties, and designer dresses—was dramatic.

At the elevator, Jackie invited Natalie and Bud back to her house for drinks. Natalie replied, "Thanks, but no thanks."

Natalie was driving back to her house when Bud made a comment.

"What a bunch of shitheads," Bud called her friends.

"Yes, they are." Natalie agreed. "They do nothing but fly to Europe on skiing trips and complain about how difficult it is to find good powder."

"It must be fun," Bud said, sarcastically. "But I'd like to see Europe one day."

"Would you?" Natalie said.

- 36 -

The next two weeks were much of the same: Bud and Natalie taking the boat out, going to the beach, eating out, going to The Chateau. Bud was never without money. Natalie knew instinctively when he was low on cash and bills would mysteriously appear near his wallet. They used his MG during the day, her T-Bird at night. They went to Omar's and The Shack twice—The Box was off limits. Being with Natalie and making love to Natalie was exciting. Bud was living the dream life.

Mike came up to him on the beach one day. There was a letter for him at The Box. Bev handed it to him avoiding eye contact. Both were uncomfortable. He stepped outside to read it.

Dear Son,

I wish you would write more often. I worry about you. I can't hope but pray you are doing well. Your father is fine and so am I. Everyone asks about you. I tell them you are all right. I saw Sheila's mother the other day. She said Sheila went to New York to study acting.

Bud's heart jumped. Perspiration appeared on his brow. He looked up nervously, catching his breath. The shock of what he just read was overwhelming. It had never entered his mind that Sheila was that adventurous. It dawned on him that he really didn't know her.

Mrs. Gray said if you wanted her address to write to her, she would give it to you. Please take care of yourself and let me hear from you soon.

Mother

He put the letter in his bathing suit and returned to the beach. His mind was whirling in confusion and self-doubt.

"Hey, what's the matter? You look like death warmed over," Natalie said.

"Nothing. Just a letter from home. I should write." He watched the waves breaking on the beach, lost in thought.

"Call from the house," Natalie said.

"Yeah, I think I will," he said.

They left the beach as the sun was disappearing. Bud's thoughts were on home. Natalie asked for a gin and tonic as she headed for a shower. Bud took a long pull on a bottle of Scotch. Fifteen minutes later, dressed in light blue capri slacks and a matching transparent top, Natalie took her drink and sat beside Bud on the couch. Her naked breasts were visible through the blouse. By the third drink, Bud was drowsy.

"What did your mother say?" Natalie asked.

"Nothing. The usual. Write and let me know how you are."

"I'm starving. Why don't you surprise me in the cooking department?" Natalie joked.

"I thought you said you didn't like my cooking."

"I didn't say that. I said, I didn't like the way you made eggs."

"Oh. In that case Chef Turner will surprise you."

He took two small steaks from the fridge, put them on the counter. Alongside them he put two baking potatoes and two ears of corn. Before lighting the indoor grill, he went back for his beer. Natalie reached up, drew him down and kissed him passionately. The steaks, potatoes, and corn went uneaten.

- 37 -

Bud and Natalie were with the beach crowd at Omar's talking about the upcoming tourist season. Marge, Delores, and Judy had gotten jobs at hotels along the beach. It was going to be a hell of a season. Hotels and motels were already booked. Almost every available room within three blocks of the beach had also been booked. Between the college kids coming for Spring Break and the winter vacationers, there wouldn't be room to walk or places to eat. The beach would be a vast blanket of tourists.

The combo was playing Wilson Pickett's, "The Letter." Everyone got up to dance. The air was stale and humid, cigarette smoke thick. Sweat drenched T-shirts. There was a wild, carefree attitude as though the beach crowd was trying to squeeze as much abandonment into the few remaining days of the off season before the tourists showed up.

Pitchers of beer appeared and disappeared in minutes. The atmosphere was frantic. Bud's eyes started to haze. The noise was deafening. The only way to be heard was to shout.

Johnny yelled at the waitress, "Let money bags get the next round! He's loaded!"

"Yeah, he has a bank with him all the time!" Mike shouted.

The words stunned Bud. He reached over and grabbed Johnny by his T-shirt.

"You fucking bastard!" Bud yelled.

Johnny wrenched free of Bud's hand. Mike was quickly up, holding Bud back as Johnny squared off for a fight. Natalie grabbed

Bud's arm to pull him back down. He pulled away and stormed out. Natalie followed him.

He drove in silence. At the house, he slammed the car door shut, rattling the window.

"That son of a bitch!" he shouted.

"Don't worry about it. He had too much to drink," Natalie said.

Bud faced her. "He's right. I do have a bank with me all the time. You."

Natalie lit a cigarette. "You're tired. Why don't we go to sleep? It'll all be forgotten tomorrow."

"Forgotten! Are you kidding? They think I'm being kept by you."

She unconsciously arched her eyebrows.

"I even know it. What the hell is going on? I can't take any more of this."

"Bud, you're not being kept," she said.

"What the hell do you call it then? I haven't made a dime in months. You give me everything. What do you think I am?" he asked her.

"I don't think you're anything."

He glared at her.

She caught herself. "I didn't mean that the way it sounded."

"Yes, you did. You know damn well I'm being kept. In fact, you like it. You like having a big cock around anytime you want it."

She sipped her drink. Her indifference obvious.

"And what the hell do I do around here except fuck and fix drinks. You don't give anything of yourself. You just want a body. Any body."

"I don't just want any body," Natalie told him. "Do you think you're God's gift? Do you? Don't stand there and take out your frustrations on me. I'm not the one asking you to wait on me. You want to. You feel it's the only way you can pay me back, because I give you money and let you sleep here. It's your frustration, not me, you're pissed off about. Don't tell me that it's all my fault. You started cooking. You started waiting on me. I didn't ask you to. What the hell do you think I have a maid for? To congratulate you on the way you keep house?" she said, condescendingly. "Don't take it all out on me."

"Why didn't you say something? Why did you let it go on?" Bud said. "The first night we went out you told me not to worry about money. You had a ball showing me off to your friends—your big new cock. They weren't impressed. They couldn't care less, as you say."

"Yes, they …" She stopped, caught on her own petard. "Bud, let's not fight. Have a drink and get me one too. We're just tired."

"Get your own fucking drink. I'm giving up being a butler," he said and passed her on the way to collect his things. She ran down the hall after him.

"Okay, you bastard. Leave. I hope you drop dead. If you lose me, you'll lose a life you can only dream about!" she yelled, hatefully.

He brushed past her, jumped into his MG, peeling rubber as he sped out of the driveway. Under his breath he whispered, "Bitch."

- 38 -

The next day, after sleeping on the beach that night, Bud bought the *Sun Sentinel*. The want ads were full of white-collar vacancies. In a box at the bottom of one of the pages was an ad that read, "Car Salesmen Needed. No Experience." He pulled into Sunrise Auto ten minutes later. After a brief interview, he was told to come back tomorrow morning at seven thirty and wear casual clothes, but not too casual.

He had a crumpled twenty-dollar bill in his pocket. He had to find a cheap room. Over on Oakland was his best bet. At the intersection of A1A and Sunrise, Dough pulled up alongside him.

"Pull over, I want to talk to you," Dough called.

He parked at the side of the road. They got out of their cars and sat on the bumper of Dough's, facing the ocean.

"Where are you off to?" Dough asked.

"I was just going to look for a room," Bud said.

Dough had a good idea of what happened. "Why don't you move in with me? There's the couch and the rent's cheap."

"Nah, I'm okay. Anyhow, I still owe you over a hundred bucks. I got a job over at Sunrise Auto. I can hold out until my first paycheck."

"Forget the money for now. You just bring your stuff over to my place and we'll talk about it."

Bud declined the invitation again, but Dough was adamant. "Your ass in that MG and over to my place. Pronto," Dough insisted.

At Dough's Bud put all his things in one of the closets. They didn't take up much space.

"What time do you start?" Dough asked.

"Seven thirty tomorrow morning," Bud said.

Dough threw him a beer. He waited for Bud to start talking. He felt he wanted to. After an awkward silence, Bud told him what happened. Dough didn't comment; he listened, knowing the feeling.

Dough invited him over to the pool. Bud said he wanted some time alone. He'd see him later. He read the employees' brochure from Sunrise Auto. He was expected to be on time, deport himself in a hospitable manner, and always be presentable in his appearance. There was to be one orientation class: "Methods and Procedures to Selling." He put his bathing suit on and went to the beach.

The first person he saw was Johnny.

"Sorry about last night," Bud said.

"I was drunk. I didn't mean anything," Johnny said.

"It was true. It opened my eyes."

"What happened? You two didn't have a fight, did you?" Johnny said, desperation creeping into his words.

Bud nodded.

"Christ, Bud, it might have been true, but every guy on the beach would love to have that kind of set up. I didn't mean you were sponging. You're the envy of every beach bum. They've had their eye on Nat for months. She just never picked any of us."

Bud couldn't believe what he was hearing. He looked closely at Johnny to see if he was bullshitting. The sincerity in his eyes confirmed he was telling the truth.

"The way you said it. The ridicule … the whole thing …" Bud was lost for words.

"I was drunk. I was really wishing it were me. Every guy on the beach would've changed places with you in a second."

"Maybe you can pick up where I left off? I split last night."

"Get on your horse and ride right back. She's probably waiting."

"I don't think so. It wouldn't be the same."

"Think about it. It's a good thing. I hate to see you lose it. I have to split. See you later," Johnny said, as he ambled off down the beach.

So Bud was the envy of the beach bums! That made him feel good. If he had a good thing and let it go, he could always find another. This was Ft. Lauderdale. Fun in the sun. There must be more Natalies around. Her friends at the golf club for starters. He wouldn't go to the car joint tomorrow. He ran into the surf feeling reborn.

Marge came by and they went to her place, had coffee, and fucked like bunnies. After he went to Dough's and opened a beer. Dough came in a short time later.

"Getting an early night so you'll be fresh for the new job?" Dough asked.

"I'm not taking the job. It's not the greatest," Bud said.

"Why? What changed your mind?"

"Nothing really. I just don't like waking up early," he lied.

"You woke up early when you were a lifeguard."

"That was different."

Dough didn't say anything. He sat on the couch thinking how Bud had changed, from a young callow kid to a destructive, avaricious beach bum. Bud graduated into what Dough was afraid of: nihilism. Maybe even worse since he didn't have a job. If Natalie was any indication, Bud was on the road to becoming a gigolo. It was very tempting and easy to fall into. How would he persuade him to leave? How could he convince him that what he was going to do would be a waste of his life? But if he pushed right now, he might just harden Bud's determination. It saddened him to think he might not be persuasive enough. He'd give it a shot anyhow.

"If I were you, Bud, I'd get my ass out of here. There's nothing here for you. There's no future in it."

"No? You did pretty well.

"Yeah, but look what I lost."

"That won't happen to me. After all, I'm not married," Bud said.

"One day you might want to be."

"I'll cross that bridge when I get to it."

Dough had no answer to that. If his life was looked upon as a success, then Bud was deluding himself. Nothing Dough could say would change his mind.

Come on, I'll buy you a beer," Bud said. "I want to celebrate."

"What?"

"Freedom. I don't know. Just celebrate."

- 39 -

They went to The Box. Bev wasn't there. She was off already. By nine o'clock, they were drunk. They were hanging onto each other like limp pieces of wallpaper.

"The Shack," Dough said.

They jumped in Dough's jeep, driving recklessly through Dania, weaving across the double white line on US 1. Horns beeped and honked incessantly.

By twelve, they could barely stand. Bob tried to get them to stop, but they wouldn't hear of it. Mike and Jake came in and also tried to get them to stop. They ignored them, both in their own deleterious world. Mike coached Bud away from Dough. He suggested he drive Bud back to Ft. Lauderdale. Bud waved him off, telling him he was fine.

"No help necessary," Bud said.

Marge, Judy, and Bev came in. Before she knew what was happening, Bud slung his arms over Bev's shoulders, leading her to the bar.

"One beer for my friend," he said.

"Bud, you're drunk," she said.

"Who? Me? I'm not drunk. I'm plastered," he said, laughing loudly.

Delores and Johnny came in.

"When are you leaving?" Delores said.

"Leaving? I'm not leaving." Bud said.

"I am," Bev said.

"Ah, you're not leaving. You're going to have another beer." He yelled for another.

The Slow Wave

Delores whispered in Bud's ear, "Bev is leaving Lauderdale."

He couldn't comprehend what she was saying. "Where's she going? Miami for a football game?" he slurred.

"She's going home," Delores said.

"Home," he repeated. Of course she was going home. She lives in Ft. Lauderdale.

He stumbled over to Dough who was arm wrestling with Bob, sweating profusely under the strain. Bob's arm gave under Dough's drunken Herculean power and slammed into the bar.

"That's one Scotch. Let's go for another," Dough said.

"No, you win," Bob said. He went to the other end of the bar, leaving Bud and Dough to their own devices.

"Bud, let's get the hell out of here. I feel like a swim," Dough said.

"Okay."

"But first I have to finish this. I just beat Bob in a fight of guts." He downed the Scotch and threw his arm around Bud's neck, weaving both toward the door.

"Bud, you're all right. I like you. But I think you're nuts. I think you better get your ass the hell out of Lauderdale before you wind up like me, a thirty-seven-year-old lifeguard who's waterlogged."

They climbed into the jeep.

Bud was laughing. Dough was funny. A thirty-seven-year waterlogged something. That was funny.

Bud shouted, "Wait! I forgot my cigs." He jumped out of the jeep and ran back into the Shack. Dough put the jeep in gear and shot out of the parking lot, burning rubber as he did. US 1 was a blur.

Bud stumbled out of The Shack. No Dough. "Where the hell's my friend? Where's he gone to?" He turned to go back into The Shack and collapsed.

– 40 –

The sun streamed through the windows, falling across an inert Bud. It was two thirty in the afternoon. The heat was unbearable. He painfully opened his eyes and saw a familiar face. Bev was looking down at him.

"Where am I?" he said, hoarsely.

"My place," Bev said.

"Where's Dough? I was with him last night. Where is he?" His head was pounding, his eyes burned.

Bev went to the kitchen, made instant coffee, and handed the cup to Bud.

"Thanks."

It was too hot to drink. He very carefully placed it on the table. Pain shot through him as he moved. He lay back and passed out. Hours later, with the shadows of the night filling the room, Bud woke, disoriented still. He ambled over to the bathroom, turned the shower on, and stood under it. Minutes later, he unsteadily stood in the living room, dressing. The place was empty, eerily quiet. His head was now a distant pounding echo.

The Box was empty except for Bev and Max. Cass was behind the bar. He went up to them.

"What a night. I feel like the lights went out up here." He pointed to his head.

No one said anything. They were looking at him with sad, blank expressions. He sensed something was wrong.

"What gives?" he asked.

Max went to the bar and brought back a shot glass and bottle of Scotch.

"What's this for, hair of the dog?" Bud asked.

"Dough is dead," Max said.

Bud stiffened. His belly tightened. His hands hit the sides of his legs unconsciously. He felt faint.

"You're shitting me." He tried laughing.

"No. His jeep hit a telephone poll in Dania last night after he left The Shack," Bev said, tears streaming down her face.

"Dead," Bud said. "Why wasn't I in it? I left with him."

"You came in for your cigarettes and passed out," Bev said.

His legs weakened. His body weaved. Max grabbed him before he fell. Instant images of last night appeared. Dough and him drinking. Dough winning the arm wrestling. Dough jumping in his jeep. Dough saying something about being thirty-seven. Something about being waterlogged. He started crying. Minutes later he got up and left.

Bev followed him out. "I'm leaving Bud. I'm going home. I told you last night. But you were too drunk to understand."

"Why?" he asked.

"I've had enough. I used to be a pretty good illustrator. I can go back to it." She took a deep breath of air, as if sucking in strength. "If you want to, I'd like you to come with me."

He stood there, thinking, *What would I do? What would the future be? Would it be worth it?* The phrase, "worth it" shook him to his foundation.

"No, I don't think so. But thanks."

He slowly walked across A1A. Standing on the sidewalk, he watched the rolling waves slowly wash up over the beach. A car skidded to a stop.

"Hey, Bud. Hey, Bud."

He turned. Through tears he saw Dee waving at him.

"My parents are away for the month. Why don't you follow me to my house?" she said.

Bud stared at her, understanding the offer. Out of the corner of his eye, he caught movement. Laura was walking along the beach. She found her usual bench and laid on it.

He walked toward Dee, continued past her across A1A, and got into his MG. He drove past the lonely figure of Bev standing outside The Box.

Bud collected his things from Dough's. He had a two-day drive ahead of him.

Epilogue

When he was young, he never thought of growing old.

The last time Bud saw this coastline, it was attractive Art Deco and aging nicely, virtual Xanadu, fast becoming a collegiate Gomorrah that would eventually be destroyed by greed and gentrification. The beaches were once pristine white and full of nubile youth, a distant cry from what he was observing now. What he saw now were freshly constructed skyscrapers in the new modern style and hordes of tourists feverishly searching the populated sand and surf for space.

He was seeking his past.

Gone were the old Deco homes and buildings. Instead of aging nicely, a sterile, modern-day metropolis spread out before him.

His slow, melancholy drive didn't yield architectural nostalgia, only more of what he had observed for the past few miles—transformation! If he hadn't known where he was, he would've bet his last dollar that he was somewhere else. Las Vegas, Singapore, Hong Kong came to mind. Not the Mecca for youth it once was. The proverb that the more things change, the more they remain the same would not, in anyone's stretch of the imagination, apply here.

His recollection of what was, disturbed him profoundly. The one building he recognized, only because it was in the same location as many years past, had undergone radical change. If the glaring neon "BAR" sign above the entrance proclaiming its use was not visible, he would have passed it by without the slightest recollection, surrounded as it was with tourist paraphernalia, hiding the beauty of the remaining Art Deco. Not to mention the twenty-five-story condominium towering above it. Consequently, a shiver of melancholy recognition ran through him.

After the business conference he was attending ended, he took a rental car from downtown Miami to make the short drive here. Once or twice, shivers of delight swept through him, happy memories of years past coming to mind, but the change he observed now was so complete and the shock so upsetting that he was sadly relieved to leave behind the sun-drenched coastal city of sun and surf he had known in his blithe but hedonistic youth.

THE END

Review Requested:

We'd like to know if you enjoyed the book.
Please consider leaving a review on the platform
from which you purchased the book.

Ingram Content Group UK Ltd.
Milton Keynes UK
UKHW010633220523
422140UK00004B/255